# EVIL THING
## A TALE OF THAT DE VIL WOMAN

# Evil Thing
## A Tale of That De Vil Woman
### By Serena Valentino

DISNEP · HYPERION

LOS ANGELES • NEW YORK

Designed by Alfred Giuliani
Layout and composition by Arlene Schleifer Goldberg

Printed in the United States of America
First Hardcover Edition, July 2020
10 9 8 7 6 5 4 3
ISBN 978-1-368-00903-4
FAC-021131-20288
Library of Congress Control Number: 2019953360
This book is set in 13-point Garamond 3 LT Pro.
www.disneybooks.com

*Dedicated with love to my dog Gozer*

## CHAPTER I

# CRUELLA DE VIL

I suppose I could start my story here, in Hell Hall, where all my marvelous plans were born from the darkness. But I'd rather start from the beginning, or at least close enough to give you an idea of what makes me tick. Sure, you know the story of those puppies, those wretched Dalmatians and their insipid owners, Roger and Anita. And I'm sure you even rooted for them to evade me. Me, that monster, the "devil woman" in a fur coat. But don't I deserve a chance to tell my own side of the story? The real story. It *is* fabulous, after all. Behold! The story of *me*. Cruella De Vil!

Ticktock, darlings, we're going back in time to

when I was a young girl of eleven living in my family's mansion. So prepare yourselves, dears; you're in for a wild ride.

My mama, papa, and I lived in a grand house on Belgrave Square. It was large, lurid, and magnificent, an imposing home with four massive columns supporting a terrace that looked down on the square. Our community was tucked safely away from the common London rabble on the other side. We were on *the proper side*, surrounded by many sprawling parks, creating a world that seemed to belong to us alone.

Of course, one could see the occasional servant polishing the brass on the front porches, or a nanny strolling in the park with her squealing charge. And there were the old women who sold violets on corners, and the little boys who sold the papers and delivered messages, but they were almost invisible, like wraiths. I hardly thought of them as people.

I called them "non-people." To me, they almost seemed like ghosts.

While of course my own servants were very

much alive, most of them were like silent specters, popping in and out of view only when we needed them. They weren't *real*. Or didn't seem so to me, anyway. Not like Mama and Papa. Not like me. Some of my servants seemed more real to me than others. The ones who were always in my view. The servants who weren't quite servants, but something in between a servant and a member of my family. We shall get to them in good time.

But oh, how I loved my mama and papa, and our grand house in Belgravia with its crystal chandeliers, lavish wallpapers, and shining wood floors covered in exotic rugs. And in a way I even loved our ghostlike servants moving silently and systematically through the house, taking care of our every whim. Always there. Always ready to do my bidding at the sound of a tinkling bell.

The image of our grand house shines in my memory like a light, desperately trying to lead me back home again. If only I could stand within the safety of its walls once more. To live my days as gloriously as I did when I was a child, when everything was simple. There were so many splendid days in that house. They spin around in my memory, sometimes making me dizzy with homesickness.

I spent most of my days with Miss Pricket, my governess, in the schoolroom. Miss Pricket had steered my education since I was old enough to learn how to read. She gave me lessons in French, watercolor painting, needlepoint, reading, and writing. Most girls in our social circle got their educations from their governesses. Had I been a boy I would have been sent off to boarding school, where I would have learned all manner of subjects, such as Greek mythology, history, and mathematics. Girls were expected to learn how to conduct themselves in a morning room. How to behave like proper young ladies. How to host splendid parties, plan menus, and direct conversations at dinner. And that, too, was part of the education I received from Miss Pricket. But she never said no if I expressed interest in a subject that wasn't reserved for young ladies. She encouraged my zeal for geography, for example, and let me devote as much time as I wanted to learning about the cultures and customs of different countries, because she knew I desperately wanted to travel the world when I was old enough to take such an adventure. I have such fond memories of those days. But my favorite part of each day was when I would go down to the morning room with Miss Pricket to spend a blissful hour with my mama.

One hour every day, entirely devoted to me.

My mother's passion for exquisite clothes was unwavering. She was always beautifully dressed in the latest designs. No one could hold a candle to her, not even me. And you all know how stunning I am, don't you, dears? You've seen my photos in the papers. You know of my exploits and my relentless devotion to fashion. Well, my dears, my mama was the same. She had an exciting, glamorous life, and she deserved it. She was the most beautiful and beguiling woman I ever met. She was a true lady.

She didn't *have* to make time for me, as busy as she was, but she did, at the same time each day right after my lessons with Miss Pricket. I would hold the image of my mama in my mind as I headed down our grand staircase, making my way from the schoolroom to the morning room. I had to will myself not to run down the stairs, to be a proper young lady and not squeal with delight because I was so excited to see my mama. After all, my schoolroom was a new development. It had been recently converted from the nursery, which meant I was on my way to becoming a young lady.

Miss Pricket was always there, holding my hand to make sure I behaved properly. Not that I needed her guidance in how to behave. Though I *did* need her guidance in how to dress, as I had not yet developed Mama's ingenious skill for putting together an ensemble. Before we left the schoolroom each day to be presented to Mama, Miss Pricket made sure I was fastidiously put together. I insisted on nothing less than perfection. Miss Pricket would list everything off in succession as she inspected me, checking to see if my hair, dress, and bows were all in proper order, knowing I would be mortified if my mother noticed anything out of place. I wouldn't dream of going down to the morning room without first changing into one of my prettier dresses, or before making sure my hair was in perfect ringlets.

The morning room was the room Mama preferred. It was her domain, and decorated exquisitely. It wasn't the largest room in the house; as one of the rooms on the main floor reserved for family, it was smaller but cozy and one of the most beautiful. The far wall was lined with windows, along with a set of French doors that led to the terrace, which looked down on Belgrave Square. In front of the windows was a large wooden desk where my mother did her correspondences and dealt with the daily running of the house. On the right-hand wall was the fireplace. The mantel was tastefully decorated with the precious treasures my parents had collected during their various travels around the globe: a pair of lovely jade tiger statues, a small golden clock, and a black onyx statue of Anubis, the Egyptian god and protector of ancient tombs. Anubis took the shape of a dog, and I always fancied he was a protector of dogs, until my father set me straight. And of course on the mantel were the invitation cards to dinners and parties that adorned the mantels of all the more fashionable households. Mama always had at least three invitations there on any given week.

Painted above the fireplace was a large semicircular art deco design that has been branded into my memory. When I close my eyes and think of the Belgravia house, I think of that design. I only wish I could describe it more accurately, because it's not the design I'm trying to describe as much as the feeling it evokes when I think of it. A sense of home. How does one describe that?

The feeling of home.

On the far right of the fireplace was a set of bookshelves flanked by two large potted palms, and a distance before them was a rolling tray with various decanters containing spirits, cocktail glasses, and a canister for dispensing seltzer water. Before the fireplace was a leather couch, and opposite were two leather chairs with a small round table between them. The walls were painted a dusty plum and decorated with oil paintings in ornate golden frames, portraits of austere ladies and gentlemen. They were likely relatives of my father's whose names have been lost to us.

Almost every visit to the morning room to see my mother was the same, but it took my breath away each time I saw her sitting on the leather couch, waiting for me. She was so striking, my mama. Whatever her plans were after our visit in the morning room would determine how she was dressed. Usually it was an afternoon out with friends for tea and shopping. In one of my memories she wears a lovely tea-length dress with a low sash around her hips, as was the fashion then. Her lipstick is a dusty rose color to match her dress, a striking contrast to her long, shining black hair, which she wore bundled up to look like a bob. In the evenings when she would go out, she would wear red lipstick, but never in the daytime. *Red lipstick is for evenings,* she would always say. Sometimes I still hear her advice echoing in my mind, and when I do I feel as though I am still a little girl.

One particular afternoon stands out in my mind.

To be honest, I can't say if this memory is of one day or many, all jumbled up together in my mind. Still, it shines brightly. My mother was sitting casually on the brown leather couch that was draped with a lavish red throw. I wanted to run into her arms the moment I saw her, but Miss Pricket squeezed my hand, a gentle reminder to act like a young lady. Instead, I stood patiently, waiting for her to divert her attention from the stack of letters and cards she was going through. When she finally looked up at me, I smiled my most charming smile.

"Good afternoon, Cruella, my dear," she said, putting her cheek out for me to kiss it. "I see you're wearing that red dress again."

I was mortified. Mama looked disappointed in me, and it made my stomach drop.

"I thought you liked this dress, Mama. You said so just the other day. You said it made me look pretty." My mother sighed and put down the letters she was going through.

"That's my point, my dear. I just saw you wearing it a few short days ago, yet you insist on wearing it again, when I know your closet is bursting with new dresses. A lady is never seen wearing the same dress twice, Cruella." I was livid with Miss Pricket. How could she let this happen? How could she let me wear the same dress twice?

"Miss Pricket, would you mind ringing for tea? Then, please, the both of you, do sit down. You're making me nervous hovering around me like a couple of birds."

"Of course, your ladyship." Miss Pricket pulled the cord hanging to the left of the fireplace mantel, then sat down in one of the leather chairs across from the couch where Mama and I usually sat. While we waited for our tea, Mama would always ask me the same questions in the same succession. Every single time. She never missed a beat, my mama.

"Are you minding Miss Pricket, my dear?"

"Oh yes, Mama."

"Good girl. And are you doing well with your lessons?"

"Yes, Mama. Very well. Right now I'm reading a book about a brave young princess who can talk to trees."

"Stuff and nonsense. Talking to trees, indeed. Miss Pricket, what's this folderol you're having my daughter read?"

"It's one of Cruella's adventure stories, my lady, from the book Lord De Vil gave her."

"Ah, yes. Well, I won't have her ruining her eyes, reading in the late hours."

"No, my lady. I read the stories to her in the evenings."

"Very well then. Oh, look. Jackson is here with the tea." And so he was, closely followed by Jean and Pauline, two young maids in black uniforms with white hats and aprons. I could always tell what time of day it was based on the color of the maids' uniforms. Mornings and early afternoons they were in pink, and late afternoons and evenings they wore black.

Jackson had a tray with the teapot, teacups, saucers, little plates, sugar, and cream. It was my favorite tea service, the one with the tiny red roses. Jean had sandwiches, scones, and little white cakes with pretty pink flowers on them, everything placed artfully on a standing tray with multiple tiers that she set beside Mama. Pauline, who my mama called Paulie, had a great raspberry jelly sitting prettily on a silver plate. It jiggled as she set it upon the table. "And what's this, Paulie?" Mama asked. "A special treat from Mrs. Baddeley?" Paulie gave me a sly grin as she answered my mama.

"Yes, my lady, made especially for Miss Cruella."

"Well, you'd better go down to the kitchen and thank Mrs. Baddeley after we've had our tea, Cruella. That was very thoughtful of her to send you a jelly. Though next time, Paulie, have her send it to the nursery. I don't want sticky sweets in the morning room."

"It's the schoolroom now, Mama," I said quietly.

"What's that, dear? Speak up. I won't have you acting the timid mouse," she said, eyeing the jelly like it might leap off the table and ruin the fine rug at any moment.

"It's the schoolroom now, not the nursery," I said, raising my voice a bit.

"Yes, of course, dear, but that detail is hardly worth you interrupting me. Now, you shouldn't keep Mrs. Baddeley waiting. Are you almost finished with your tea?"

Miss Pricket took my plate piled with little sandwiches and tea cakes with one hand and took my teacup by the saucer with the other, then placed them on the silver tray. "Jean will take these down to the kitchen for you, won't you, Jean? So Miss Cruella can finish them there."

"That's a lovely idea, Miss Pricket. Don't you think, Cruella? I have to dash out anyway, my dear. I shouldn't be late to meet Lady Slaptton. If I am, she will speak of nothing else until something else diverts her attention." Mama then turned to our butler. "Jackson, my coat."

"Yes, your ladyship." And out he went, with Jean and Pauline following him from the morning room with all of the tea things.

"Give your mama a kiss before she goes, Miss

Cruella," Miss Pricket said, as if I needed coaxing. But the fact was, I was taking my time. I wanted to see Mama in her fur coat.

"You can follow me to the vestibule if you'd like, Cruella, and see me off before you head down to the kitchen." Miss Pricket took my hand and walked out of the morning room into the vestibule, the main entryway. It was the grand nexus of our home. One could say it was the heart of the house. In the center of the room was a round table with a vase of flowers that were changed daily. My father often put his hat on that table when he walked in the door. It would, of course, be spirited away by his man to be cleaned before it would be returned to his room, where he would find it the next day. To the right of the main entryway was our exquisite dining room, and to the left was the grand staircase that led upstairs to a sitting room and a ballroom, and farther up still was the floor with our bedrooms. One more flight up were the servants' quarters, tucked away in the attic. At the foot of the grand staircase was the doorway that led down to the basement, where you could find the kitchen, and where the servants worked. And right across from the front doors was the morning room, the soul of the house.

Jackson and Jean were standing near the front door, waiting for us. Jackson held my mama's fur coat, and Jean held my mother's handbag, which glittered in the early evening light. After Jackson helped my mother on with her coat, she patted me on the head.

"Now be a good girl, Cruella. And don't gorge yourself on sweets no matter how forcefully Mrs. Baddeley insists. Goodbye, my darling. I won't be home for dinner." She blew me a kiss and dashed out the door, her long fur coat trailing behind her dramatically. My mother was always off to meet her friends, sometimes not returning home until the early evening. And if Father was away, or late at the House of Lords, sometimes she wouldn't come home until well after dinner, when I was already in bed.

Most days were like this.

Oh, but how I loved my special time with

Mama. An hour a day every day, for as long as I could remember. An hour devoted entirely to me. It was the highlight of my day. A memory I hold on to now in the darkness.

My time with Mama.

Beautiful Mama in her fur coats, glittering jewels, and fancy frocks. Beautiful Mama dashing off to exciting locations. She was tall, thin, and lanky, with striking black hair and eyes so dark brown that they, too, almost looked black. She had high cheekbones, with angular features any model or actress would die for. She was always dripping with diamonds and draped in glittering dresses, and, of course, her fur coats. I can see her now when I close my eyes. Shining in the darkness, like a shimmering star.

After my blissful hour with Mama in the morning room, Miss Pricket escorted me down to the kitchen to thank our cook, Mrs. Baddeley, for the jelly. She didn't always send a jelly, but when she did, Mama insisted that I be polite.

I have to be honest: Mrs. Baddeley was insufferable. She was a squat, red-faced woman with eyes that always seemed to be smiling. She was often covered in flour, and strands of hair would fall from the bun that was piled high on her head. Each time she brushed the hair out of her face, she would get more flour all over herself. She was fond of cooing at me like I was still a little girl and not a young lady, and asking me questions that were quite frankly none of her business. Why should she care what I was learning in school? Mama didn't needle me on which subjects I was taking, so why should our cook?

On my way downstairs I closed my eyes tightly, willing myself to be kind to her and bracing myself for her squealing litany of rapid-fire questions.

"Oh, Cruella! How are you doing, my girl?" she asked as soon as she heard my shoes clicking down the stairs. For an older woman, she had the keenest hearing. I swear she could hear me coming all the way from the third floor, and she'd have a jelly made and ready for me by the time I reached the basement.

"I'm very well, Mrs. Baddeley," I recited. "Thank you for the jelly, it was beautiful." Her laugh was slightly raspy, unrefined and loud. It matched her appearance all too perfectly.

"Oh, my girl, it tastes even better than it looks! Here you go," she said as she set a heaping portion on the island across from where she was rolling some dough. "Sit down, my dear. I know jellies are your favorite."

The fact was I hated jellies, but somehow she had got it into her head I loved them, and so it seemed that I would be besieged by Mrs. Baddeley's jellies for the rest of my childhood.

I sat at the stool across from her and forced down my jelly as I watched her roll the dough, a big smile on her face as she asked me her insipid questions.

"Would you like to invite some friends over for tea? How about that dear sweet girl Anita? We can make a party of it! I can make all your favorites. Doesn't Anita like lemon tarts?"

"She does, thank you," I said between delicate bites. Mama had warned me not to eat too much, after all.

"I simply can't believe how old you're getting.

Why, you will be turning twelve soon, Miss Cruella! I shall make you something special, you can be sure of that." Honestly, she wouldn't stop talking. "And it won't be long now until you're off to finishing school. Just a couple of years. Are you excited? Nervous? Oh, Cruella, you will love school, all those new friends and adventures . . ." And it went on like that for what seemed like an eternity. How impertinent. As if *she* knew what I would and would not love. She was always feigning an interest in me, Mrs. Baddeley was. It drove me to distraction. My mother didn't even ask me those questions. What made a cook think she could? But isn't that always the way with cooks, chumming it up with the children of the house? Mama told me stories about her family's cooks, how they passed her sweets and were always striking up inappropriate conversations. I know Anita adored her guardian's cook—she practically looked to her as a second mother. But that was something I never understood. I *had* a mother. A marvelous mother. What would I want with a flour-dusted woman who fussed over me almost constantly? I was polite to her, of course. I answered her questions. And I was sweet about it. (Not quite as sweet as Mrs. Baddeley's noxious jellies, but sweet nevertheless.) That's how a young lady is expected to conduct herself, so that is how I acted when I did my duty and went down to the kitchen to thank the annoying woman.

On occasion, my mother, too, would go down and speak with the cook, to remark on an exceptional meal or to thank her for impressing our guests. I think it was because she was afraid we would lose her to another house if she didn't make a fuss over her from time to time. So many of our guests remarked on Mrs. Baddeley's cooking that my mother was sure someone would snap her up. "It's not like the old days," Mama would say, "when servants were bound to a household their entire lives. They have other opportunities now. Some of them even know how to read and write. We must do our part to keep them loyal." So she would descend the stairs in her glittering gowns, looking quite out of place, to flash a thankful smile at Mrs. Baddeley and praise her like one might praise a needy little puppy.

Ah, puppies. But we'll get to that part of the story soon enough.

So I took a page from my mother's book and went down to the kitchen to thank Mrs. Baddeley when she sent me a jelly. I made sure to say that I loved the raspberry most of all. I cooed over the shape of the jelly and asked if I could see the mold in which she'd made it. This all made Mrs. Baddeley chuckle with delight. She looked like a jelly herself, jiggling and wobbling as she did so. She pulled the mold down from the high shelf and showed it to me. I pretended to find it fascinating.

"Thank you, Mrs. Baddeley. Could you perhaps use the round Bundt mold next time? The one with the little trees. I love that one."

Honestly, I didn't care in which shape my jelly was made; whatever the shape, I'd still have to choke it down. But the request made her laugh, seeming to fill her simple little heart with glee, and she believed me, the fool that she was. "I will, Miss

Cruella! And it will be another raspberry to be sure!"

"Thank you, Mrs. Baddeley," I said.

*You're a fool,* I thought.

"And how was your visit with your mother today?" she asked, looking a little sad when she did. For some reason she looked to Miss Pricket for the answer.

"She was as beautiful as ever," I said loudly, making sure she knew the answer came from me and not my governess.

"I'm sure she would spend more time with you if she could, Miss Cruella," said the cook, her hands covered in flour as she rolled the dough for the savory pie she was preparing for the servants' dinner. She had made a point of telling me that rabbit pie was Jackson's favorite. I tried not to wrinkle my nose. The last time I was down there she'd been making something called a cottage pie. I supposed the lower classes loved pies.

"We had a lovely hour together," I said, smiling through my teeth. Mrs. Baddeley and Miss Pricket shared another look.

23

It was so odd the way they'd look at each other when we talked about my mama. I decided it was because they were jealous. I mean, how could they not be? Why else would they be casting strange looks between them? My mother was a lady, and they, after all, were just *servants*.

And then, as if she could sense I might say so out loud (I never would, as it certainly wouldn't have been ladylike), Miss Pricket took my hand, signaling it was time to go back upstairs. And thank goodness she did, because it turned out we had been down there for hours.

"Come on, Miss Cruella. Shall we go upstairs and call Miss Anita to invite her over for tea tomorrow?"

"Oh yes, Miss Pricket! I would love that," I said as I got down from my stool and took Miss Pricket's hand.

As I made my way up the stairs holding Miss Pricket's hand, smiling and waving at Mrs. Baddeley, my heart felt lighter. I was ascending from the darkness of the kitchen dungeon into a world that was real, and beaming with light.

Upstairs, there was life and beauty, and not a speck of flour.

I hated visiting downstairs; it was dark and stuffy down there, and the servants looked like pale ghosts in the low light. But how could they help it, really, tucked away in the basement during the day as they were, never spending time in the sunshine. I think that is one of the reasons they didn't seem real to me.

Miss Pricket, I suppose, was *almost* real. She wasn't exactly a servant, but she wasn't part of the family, either. She didn't have her meals with the servants. And she didn't stay in the servants' quarters, tucked up in the attic with the rest of them. She had her meals either with me, if my family was out for the evening, or on a tray in her room right across the hall from mine. Miss Pricket could have almost been a lady if she'd dressed like one. And she was pretty enough, underneath her austere governess attire. Her uniform made her look so much older than she was. When I was a small child it confused me because Mama referred to her as an old maid, and it wasn't until I was older that I realized she was really quite young. She had light green eyes, ginger hair, freckled cheeks, and a slim frame. She was delicate and fragile like a lady. But she wasn't a lady.

She was an *in-between*.

When Miss Pricket and I finally made our way upstairs from the kitchen and reached the entryway, I saw our butler, Jackson, approaching the door to let someone in. Jackson was tall, gray-haired, and stoic. There was a dignity about him; he always maintained his composure. He led the household like a great general at war, except without all the shouting. Jackson never shouted. At least he never shouted upstairs.

Jackson opened the door. To my surprise, it was Mama! My heart leaped and I squealed for joy. I didn't expect her back so soon.

"Cruella, please! Conduct yourself like a lady!" said Miss Pricket, squeezing my hand.

Mama swooped into the vestibule like a movie star, her fur coat gliding around her dramatically. She was followed by several footmen laden with her many packages.

"Hello, Mama!" I said, putting my cheek out to be kissed.

"Hello, Cruella, dear!" she said. Her eyes flicked down to my dress. "I see you've been down to thank Mrs. Baddeley for the jelly. Are you just coming up from the kitchen now? Miss Pricket, look at her. Exactly how long were you down there? It looks like she baked a cake herself! I won't have a daughter of mine looking like a common cook!" I looked down at my dress, mortified. I hadn't realized. Thank goodness my mother had been thoughtful enough to bring it to my attention, unlike that wretched Mrs. Baddeley, letting me parade around like a flour-covered fool! She probably didn't think there was anything wrong with that.

"Thank you, Mama." I stepped back, realizing I was foolish to extend my flour-spattered cheek. The last thing I wanted to do was get flour all over Mama's beautiful fur coat.

"Your father will be home late this evening, so I will be dining out with the Slapttons before the opera."

"Oh." My heart fell. "I thought you changed your mind and decided to have dinner at home."

"No, my darling. I'm just home to change. You can have your meal with Miss Pricket in the nursery. I'll come in to say goodbye before I leave."

"The schoolroom, Lady De Vil," Miss Pricket reminded her quickly, with a glance in my direction. "It's now the schoolroom, not the nursery." Smiling at my mother, she added, "Speaking of which, Miss Cruella is doing very well with her studies, my lady." Mama didn't answer. It was as if Miss Pricket hadn't said anything at all. And why should Mama answer her? She hadn't directly addressed Miss Pricket. And she probably didn't care to be corrected by an in-between. I couldn't expect my mother to remember something as trivial as what a silly room was called. Even if I was quite proud to be spending my days in a schoolroom rather than a nursery.

Miss Pricket's face fell. I supposed she was upset at being ignored by Mama. Or perhaps it was because Mama was so upset by the state of my clothing. Whatever the reason for her sour look, the in-between took me by the hand and led me up the stairs. We had our usual evening together, after I was made presentable again. The highlight of the evening was Mama coming into the schoolroom to say good night before she went off for her evening plans, her glittering dress sparking in the light, her heels clicking on the hardwood floors, and her bejeweled bag dangling on her arm. Her musical voice bid me good night.

"Have a lovely night, Cruella. Sleep well," she said, blowing me a kiss. "You can come to the stairs and watch me leave if you like." And I did. I always did. I loved seeing Mama leave for an evening out.

I'd watch from the top of the stairs as her sparkly dress trailed behind her until she reached the bottom, where Jackson was waiting, holding out her long fur coat. I was breathless as I watched her go. She was the most glamorous woman I had ever seen.

How I envied those fur coats! I couldn't wait until I got my first one.

I waited until the rumble of Mama's car was too far off in the distance to hear anymore, and then I went to my bedroom.

Every night was the same. Miss Pricket brought me some cocoa, and we chatted about our day as I drank it. She read to me, and then we made our plans for the next day before she tucked me in. "Should we invite Anita over tomorrow? It's been a while since we've seen her."

"Yes," I said sleepily. "I would love that." It was true. She had been traveling with her family over the summer, so it had been some time since we'd been together. Anita was my best friend, and I had missed her desperately while she had been away. I'd known Anita for as long as I could remember. She was the ward of one of my father's colleagues and best friends at the House of Lords, and even though Mama didn't think she was a suitable friend for me because she wasn't born into a high society family like I was, Papa thought she was a good influence and always insisted she be invited to our family trips and gatherings. Growing up, she was like a sister to me.

Even though Lord Snotton let her live in his home, she wasn't to be a proper lady herself, not like me. Anita wouldn't be presented to society. The most Anita could possibly expect was an exceptional education so she could go on to become a nanny or governess in a wealthy household, unless her guardians managed to find a suitable match with a gentleman who didn't mind her lack of family connections. She could, of course, decide to venture out on her own and become a shopgirl or typist. But why would she want to do that?

It reminded me of that Jane Austen story, oh, what was it called? The one about the two sisters: one married for love and the other married sensibly. And of course the one who married for love was poor, and had to send one of her daughters to live with her sister who had married sensibly. That's Anita's story in a nutshell—except Anita's guardian doesn't have a handsome son for her to fall in love with and marry. They had two daughters who went out of their way to show Anita she was below them. I wonder if, had I not gotten to love Anita the way I did from such a young age, before my mother told me about her background, I would have felt the same as those wretched Snotton girls. I guess I'll never know.

Anita was really just a step above an in-between. But she was my best friend and my favorite companion. I didn't care about her family or her lack of connections. She was the sweetest person I knew. And I loved her.

After we discussed having Anita over for tea, Miss Pricket suggested we read from my favorite book of fairy tales, as was our usual custom in the evenings.

"Should we read a bit about Princess Tulip before you go to sleep? I think we left off right as she was about to talk with the Rock Giants to help her and the Tree Lords protect the Fairylands from a terrible threat."

"I think I'm too tired for stories this evening, Miss Pricket." My eyelids were starting to droop, and I was distracted by something. "Do you understand why Mama doesn't like Anita? Is it really because of her family?"

"I really couldn't say, Miss Cruella." I knew that

was Miss Pricket's way of saying she'd prefer *not* to say, and I respected her for not speaking out against my mama. Though I wouldn't have minded if she had, because as much as I loved her, I didn't understand her distaste for Anita.

"I overheard Mama and Papa arguing about Anita, and Mama said the strangest thing. She said, 'Anita makes me feel like something is stalking my home, circling it, and scratching at its walls. I wish it was a less disturbing feeling.' What do you think she means by that, Miss Pricket?"

"You shouldn't be eavesdropping on your parents, Miss Cruella," Miss Pricket scolded gently. "It isn't ladylike." I yawned. Sometimes it was quite easy to be unladylike without even knowing it. So I changed the subject.

"Mama looked lovely this evening, didn't she, Miss Pricket? Aren't I the luckiest of girls to have such a beautiful mama?"

"Yes, she looked very lovely, Miss Cruella," she said.

"And aren't I the luckiest girl?" I prodded. She

hadn't answered that part of my question. She just sat there with the saddest look on her face. For some reason Miss Pricket always looked sad when we spoke of my mama. And she looked especially sad in the evenings. I smiled at the woman when she kissed my cheek good night, but I felt sad for her. What a lonely life she must have had. Spending her days with a child who wasn't hers, eating most of her meals alone. No family or friends of her own to love or care for her. I supposed I was the only one, in my own way, who did.

"Good night, Miss Pricket," I said with a smile, hoping it would cheer her expression, which remained fixed no matter how hard I tried.

But then something surprising happened. Her face transformed after all. "Oh! Cruella! I'm so sorry I forgot. Your mother left some gifts for you on the vanity. Look!" She dashed over to the vanity, bringing the boxes to the bed so I could open them. One box held a beautiful red dress with a matching belt. A smaller box contained shoes and a little clutch purse. The last box I opened was the biggest, and it contained the most magnificent gift of all: a white fur coat with a black collar. I popped out of bed and put it on at once. Even over my nightgown, the coat made me look glamourous.

I looked exactly like Mama. I finally had a fur coat of my very own. And I just *knew* this was the beginning of an important phase in my life. I was on my way to becoming a glamorous lady. Just like Mama.

"See, Miss Cruella, your mother *does* think of you. I think she loves you very much," said Miss Pricket. But the look in her eyes made me feel she was trying harder to convince herself than she was trying to convince me. I didn't need convincing. I knew my mama loved me.

I turned away from the mirror and gave Miss Pricket a strange look. "What a funny thing to say, Miss Pricket. Of course Mama loves me. Look at this beautiful coat!" Miss Pricket nodded, but her smile looked sad as she put away my gifts.

"Why are you so sad?" I asked her. I suppose I felt a little bad for her. She smiled again but didn't answer. That's the thing about in-betweens like Miss Pricket. Because they're almost real, you *almost* feel bad for them. You almost like them. But I never did find out what made her so sad. Our conversation was interrupted that evening before she could tell me, because suddenly there was a knock at the door.

"Cruella?" The voice I heard was deep, soft, and questioning.

"Papa? Come in!" I called back. He opened the door a crack, peering in playfully. He wore the same mischievous smile that often greeted me in the evening right before bed. I had the most handsome papa of any of my friends, with his dark hair and wide movie star grin. And he always had a smile for me. He wasn't one of those stuffy lords, the sort that looked like a giant walrus or stodgy bird. He was handsome and always smiling. Looking back, I do think my mama wished he were a little more serious. Maybe even a little stuffier. I know now she didn't appreciate that he encouraged my friendship with Anita, or that he didn't mind when I stayed up all night reading my fairy stories. And I know she didn't like the funny faces he would make at the dinner table to make me laugh. But for my part, I thought he was delightful.

I could tell Miss Pricket always felt like an intruder when Papa would swoop in for an evening chat before bed, if he made it home in time. She would awkwardly excuse herself and skitter away, more like one of the non-people than the in-between she was. It always made me laugh to see her slink off before Papa would plop down on the edge of the bed with a dramatic thump. He wasn't a bumbling man, but with me, he liked to pretend he was. It was our special thing. "And how is my girl?" he asked.

"Very well, Papa. I had a lovely day with Mama."

"You saw her today?" Papa could be so forgetful sometimes. He always seemed surprised when I told him Mama spent the day with me, even though he knew she spent an hour each day with me after my lessons.

"I did, Papa. I saw her for tea like we do every day. We had a marvelous time!"

"Did you, my girl? A marvelous time? Well,

that's very good to hear, Cruella dear." His eyes landed on the empty boxes at the foot of the bed with a frown. "I see your mother went out shopping again." I suddenly felt irritated with Miss Pricket for not taking them away. "What did she buy you this time?" he asked, looking a little cross.

"Oh, Father! Mother got me the most topping white fur coat!" I leaped out of bed and tried the coat on for him, twirling around in the mirror. "Don't I look just like her?"

"Yes, Cruella. I'm afraid you do."

He looked at me in such a strange way that I stopped twirling abruptly. Had I made him angry? "Papa, are you cross with me?" He scooped me up, twirling me around in circles.

"No, my darling. I'm not cross with you. You look lovely. Let's dance together." We danced around my room, which made us both laugh so hard we had to stop and catch our breath. Then he reached into his pocket, pulling out a small parcel wrapped in brown paper and tied with twine. "Well, I have something for you as well, my dear. It's not a fur coat, but they do come with an interesting story I think you'll appreciate."

Father rarely brought me gifts. He brought me silly smiles, conversation, and affection almost every evening, but he rarely brought me gifts. He had so little time to show me he loved me, busy as he was at the House of Lords. Unlike Mama, who was almost always bringing me home something beautiful.

"Oh, Papa!" I cried, ripping at the paper. The scraps made my white bedspread look like it was covered in brown polka dots. "I'm sorry I didn't have time to wrap it prettily," he said. "He was an interesting sort of man, the proprietor of the antique shop, not the sort who offers pretty boxes and bows." I didn't care. I could hardly wait to see what it was. But my smiled faded when I opened the box: a pair of round jade earrings. They were dull green and unremarkable.

"Thank you, Papa," I said, smiling again with some effort. Compared to the fur coat Mama had given me, it was hardly a gift at all. I think that was the moment I realized my father didn't love me after all—or at least not as much as I thought he did. If he loved me, he would have gotten me something truly beautiful. Like Mama always did.

"Cruella, my dear, I haven't told you the best part. These earrings were found in a real pirate chest!" My eyes widened. *This* was an interesting development.

"Really?"

"Yes, my dear. He was a great pirate! He stole a chest of treasures from a far-off and magical land. Remember that book I got you? The one with the strange fairy tales? Apparently the book and the earrings come from the same magical place."

"That *is* interesting!" And it was. I loved tales of fantasy and adventure. The idea of a pirate's treasure filled my heart with wonder. But I couldn't bring myself to be excited about his gift. I could see his face falling as he realized I didn't love the earrings, but he continued.

"This is the *most* interesting part, my dear. It's rumored the treasure was cursed by foul sorceresses, nasty fairies, or the like. Can you imagine?" I tried to get excited about the gift's supposedly magical history. I really did. But I was too disappointed about the boring earrings. It's not like *I* was on the pirate ship having the adventure. I would have preferred that, to be honest.

"So you got me cursed earrings?"

My father laughed. "Well, of course they're not actually cursed, Cruella. There's no such thing as curses, not really. But you loved the book of fairy tales I got you, so I thought you would enjoy the story nevertheless. Aren't you and Miss Pricket always reading about that adventurous princess, what's her name?"

"Princess Tulip," I said.

"Yes, that's her name. I knew you loved her stories, so when I heard the story of the earrings, well, I just had to get them for you." He sighed. "Even if they did cost a fortune."

*A fortune?* Why hadn't he mentioned that before? Well, *this* was another story altogether. I looked at them again, considering, and decided I liked them after all. No, I decided I *loved* them! And I chided myself for thinking my papa didn't love me.

"I love them, Papa! Thank you!" I said, wrapping my arms around his neck. His smiled faded a little. I didn't know why.

"You can be very much like your mother, Cruella," he said.

And I thought that was the sweetest thing he could have ever said to me.

## CHAPTER II

# THE LAST DE VIL

Ticktock, darlings! We can't dwell in the past forever. But that's exactly what I'm doing, isn't it, in telling you my story? This chapter is hard for me, my dears. We are moving forward in time five years, to the summer I was sixteen, when my life changed forever in so many unforeseeable ways.

In the weeks before and after my father's death, Anita was my sole companion. Mama was off visiting her sister when Papa became ill, and we were having a heck of a time trying to reach her so we could let her know she should come home . . . Miss Pricket was away, too, tending to her sick aunt. I don't know what I would have done if Anita wasn't with me in those dark days.

His illness came on suddenly and without warning. My father's Clark Gable smile and bright flashing eyes became dim and faded. He wasn't the man I knew, the man who sat with me in the evenings before I went to sleep and brought me books of fairy tales and adventures, or priceless jade earrings from distant enchanted lands. The man who danced with me in my bedroom and made me laugh at the most inappropriate times. He was a shadow of himself, and I was afraid to see him like that. The doctor said his heart was weak, and it broke mine to see him so fragile and so pale. I wanted to remember him as strong, laughing, and cheeky.

When the doctor finally emerged from Papa's room, I jumped. He lowered his eyes, and that's when he told me.

"I'm sorry, Cruella," he said.

I stood outside of his bedroom door for what felt like an eternity after the doctor left. After he told me my papa would die. I couldn't fathom it. And I couldn't bring myself to face him. I couldn't let him see the look of grief on my face. I wanted to be strong for him, but I couldn't do it.

Then Anita appeared, like an angel. Ever since she was a little girl she seemed angelic to me with her small features, light hair, and sharp little nose. If you didn't know better, you'd think she was a lady. A *real* lady. And to me she was. The only things that gave her away were her bookishness, and the smart and efficient way she dressed. Anita wasn't in for frills. She dressed sensibly, but she still managed to look stylish in her simple, light blue A-line skirt and pink blouse. She had been down in the kitchen with the servants arranging for the evening meal and generally acting in my mother's place so I would be free to focus on my papa.

"Cruella, what are you doing? Are you okay?" she asked. Anita was taking care of everyone. Not only the servants, by keeping them informed and reassuring them, but me as well. I don't know how she did it all.

"The doctor just left, Anita. He said . . ." She put her hand on my arm softly. She could tell I was about to cry.

"I know, Cruella, he told me," she said, trying not to cry herself. "You must be devastated. How is your father doing now? Is he sleeping?"

"I haven't been in since the doctor left. I can't go in there, Anita. I can't face him." I was so afraid to see my father so frail. Perhaps if Mama had been there I could have been braver, but I couldn't find the courage to say goodbye to him. I couldn't face that he was actually leaving us.

"Of course you can, Cruella. You have to," said Anita, squeezing my arm. "He loves you so much, Cruella. And I know you love him."

"I wish Mama was here. Has Jackson tried calling again? She will be devastated if she . . ." Anita gave me a weak smile. She knew my mother would be grief-stricken if she wasn't able to say goodbye.

"Oh, Cruella, I know. But even if he did reach her I don't think she would be home in time. At least that's how the doctor made it sound. I was so afraid that is what he would say. But Cruella, you have to be brave. You're the strongest girl I know, and you have to be strong for your papa. Your mama isn't here, and he needs you." She took my hand sweetly, but I could feel her strength even in her light touch. I felt she was the strongest person I knew, aside from my mama. How else could she endure her life as it was, living between worlds, not fitting in with the servants downstairs or with the family upstairs? How else could she have taken my mama's place and helped me through my papa's illness? As far I was concerned, she was my family. "Go now, Cruella. Kiss your father before it's too late. Tell him you love him. Tell him all the things you ever wanted him to know. Let him take your sweet words with him to a place you cannot follow." I wanted to cry right then. Anita's words touched me so deeply. But I had to be brave for my poor papa. I had to be strong.

His room was dark and stuffy. Not a place for such a great man to spend his final hours. In the dim light, I could hardly see him sleeping in his bed when I entered the room. His nurse was sitting in a chair nearby, dozing. A tiny beam of light from a small opening in the curtains reflected off her white uniform. She started awake when I opened the curtains, infusing the room with light.

"Miss Cruella! What are you doing? You will wake your father!" The groggy nurse blinked at the bright light with a very sour look on her face.

"It's dreary in here," I said, looking around the room. "Why don't you make yourself useful and get the small record player from my father's study and bring it in here?" The nurse looked shocked at my tone. I was a little shocked at it, too, to be honest. It just came out of me with no warning. But I had a plan.

"Excuse me?" was all the nurse could muster, blinking at me over and over and shielding her eyes from the sunlight that now poured into the room.

"Listen carefully," I said, speaking concisely. "Go into my father's study, find the small record player, and bring it here. I won't repeat myself again." I said it all very slowly so the dim-witted nurse would understand. But still she looked at me, puzzled.

"I'm paid to be a nurse, Miss Cruella. Not a

servant." The jumped-up little nurse wasn't having it. Well, neither was I.

"I see. Well, I doubt we're paying you to fall asleep on the job! So if you can't make yourself useful and get me that record player, then I suppose I will have to dismiss you. It's up to you. You can be of some use or leave. It's very simple." The woman went out of the room, and I rang the servants' bell, not sure if she was coming back with the record player or not.

"Cruella, what are you up to? Causing mayhem and mischief as usual?" It was my papa. My little spat with the nurse had roused him. He looked so small to me in his bed. So frail. It broke my heart.

"Papa! I'm sorry I woke you." And then I saw it, his mischievous smile. My papa was still in there. He hadn't completely faded away. "Oh, Papa, let me help you." I went to the bed to help him up as Jackson came into the room.

"Miss Cruella, let me do that," he said as he helped my papa sit up in bed, putting pillows behind his head.

"There, isn't that better, Papa? I have Mrs.

Baddeley making you something special in the kitchen."

"Thank you, my dear," he said with his sweet cheeky smile.

"Miss Cruella." A timid voice came from the doorway. "Did you ask the nurse to bring your father's record player in here?" Our housemaid Paulie was standing at the door, apprehensively holding the record player.

"Yes, Paulie. Put it over there on the dresser, and tell Mrs. Baddeley my father is ready for his breakfast."

"Yes, Miss Cruella." She placed the record player on the dresser as I asked, then paused. "I hope you don't mind my saying so, but the nurse is making quite a fuss in the entryway. I think she is leaving." Before I could say I was happy to see that horrible nurse go, Paulie quickly left the room.

Jackson cleared his throat. "Lord De Vil, is there anything else I can do?" The silent, strong, and stoic Jackson was standing there at the ready, sturdy as ever. He was our family's rock.

"No, Jackson. I think Cruella has it all in hand."
Papa flashed his smile at me.

"Thank you, Jackson," I said. "That will be all."
I went about the room opening all the curtains
and turning on the record player. Papa's favorite
record was already on the turntable. It was one of
his American jazz records, the ones Mama detested,
so he always listened to them while he was alone
in his study. "We can't have you withering away
in a dark and dreary room, now can we? We need a
little life in here." Papa smiled again and reached
out his hand.

"Come here, Cruella. Come sit with me on the
bed," he said. But I didn't want to. I knew if I sat
with him I would cry. As long as I was busying
myself around the room, as long as I had something
to do, I could hold my composure. But I went to
him anyway and tried my best to keep the tears from
flooding down my face.

"Thank you, my dear," he said. He was too weak
to say more. I could tell it was a struggle to sit
up, but what I wanted more than anything in that

moment was to dance with him to his favorite song.

"I wish we could dance together, Papa. One last time."

He laughed. "Like we used to in your room? I would love that, my dear. I'm so sorry I won't be here to dance with you at your wedding."

"I'm not getting married, Papa," I said, but I could tell he didn't believe me.

"Well, not now, my Cruella, but one day you will. And I only wish I could be there to see it." I couldn't hold my tears in any longer. "Don't cry, my sweet girl. Come on, help me to my feet, my strong girl, and we will dance."

"Papa, no! You can't."

"I am more stubborn than you, my girl. Where do you think you got it from? Now help me up. I want to dance with my daughter."

And so we danced, as we might have on my wedding day, spinning in slow circles and swaying back and forth until he was too weak to stand. As I was about to help him back to his bed, the nurse bustled into the room.

"What is the meaning of this? Lord De Vil, I must insist you get back into bed. What were you thinking, Miss Cruella? This is very irresponsible of you. You're endangering your father's life!" I glared at her. In that moment, there was no one I hated more. I felt myself fill with rage.

"Come on, Papa, let's get you back onto the bed. I need to go into the hall and speak to the nurse." After I helped my father and got him settled, I took that horrible girl by the arm and led her into the hallway. "I thought you were leaving. How dare you speak to me like that? I am a lady. I want you to leave this house at once!"

"I will not leave. Your father's well-being is my responsibility."

"I am taking care of my father. You are dismissed! Now leave!"

"Taking care of him indeed! Opening curtains, playing loud music, and dancing—with his heart! You are going to send him to his grave."

"He was already on his way. I want to make sure his journey is a happy one. Not dull and dreary,

having to look upon your sullen face. Now get out!"
And off she went, complaining as she left, like the
fool she was. I was relieved to see her go.

As I was about to go back into my papa's room, I
thought I heard my mother's voice down in the entryway. I ran to the landing to see if it was really her.
I had lost hope she would come home before Papa
passed. "Mama! Up here. Come quickly!" I said, calling from the top landing down to her. She looked up
at me, startled, her attention briefly diverted from
the wretched nurse, who was gesticulating angrily.
My mother's startled expression turned to wrath as
she looked at me, and my heart sank.

She rushed up the stairs. I had never seen her
rush anywhere, not once in my entire life. She was in
a fit of panic and rage. "Cruella! What is this I hear
about you causing havoc in your father's sickroom?
And forcing him to dance? I can't even look at
you! Go to your room and stay there until I've sent
for you." I just stood there in shock, not moving.
"Cruella, go now or I will slap you." And she pushed
past me into Papa's room. I didn't dare follow her

in. I knew she would make good on her threat. I wasn't sure what that damnable nurse had told her, but I didn't imagine it cast me in the most favorable light. I heard my father's music abruptly stop with the ugly sound of the needle scratching the record. And then came my mother's scream.

Papa had died, and I was sure my mother blamed me.

❖ ❖ ❖ ❖

My mother decided to travel the world after the reading of my father's will, and I didn't blame her. She was heartbroken. My father's death was so unexpected. For my mother, one day he was with us and the next he was gone. She wasn't even able to say goodbye. By the time she was done berating me for all the hateful lies the nurse had told her, my father had quietly slipped away from us. My mother was in shock, and so was I. It was strange living in a world without Papa. I missed his nightly visits and our talks, and I missed his laugh most of all.

And his smile. Oh, how I missed his mischievous smile. I must have sat at my vanity for an hour trying to decide if I wanted to wear the jade earrings Papa gave me to his funeral. I imaged it would make him smile to see me wearing them. But when I put them on, the oddest feeling came over me. It was probably all in my mind, but they made me feel so odd, so unlike myself. And I was already feeling out of sorts, trying to get used to living in this new world without Papa. In the end I decided not to wear them.

Our solicitor came by the evening after the funeral to read Papa's will. He was a funny little man, Sir Huntley. He had a round face with small round spectacles, and his jowls jiggled when he spoke. We sat in the morning room, silently watching him go through his papers until he finally arrived at the papers he was looking for. He cleared his throat and began reading.

"'I, Lord De Vil, being of sound mind and body—'" My mother cut Sir Huntley off. "Please, Sir Huntley, if you don't mind, just get on with it." Sir Huntley cleared his throat again, shuffling the papers a little more.

"Very well, Lady De Vil, if that's what you'd prefer. Your husband, Lord De Vil, has left the entirety of his fortune in trust to his daughter, of which I am to be executor until her twenty-fifth birthday." The man looked like he might pop with nervousness. Or perhaps he was fearing my mother might explode with anger. I could see by the look on his face he was expecting some sort of tantrum. Some sort of theatrics. But my mother was, at least for the moment, containing her outrage. She just sat there looking at him silently. I don't know if she was in shock or disbelief. "Lady De Vil, did you hear me?" And then it happened. The explosion he had clearly been bracing himself for.

"Of course I heard you. And what am I to do? What am I expected to do? How am I supposed to live? Can you tell me that?" My mother had startled the man so violently it made his jowls quiver again, but he bravely continued.

"Lord De Vil has made provisions for you in his will. You will be given a lifetime yearly allowance."

"And the house, its possessions?" she demanded.

She stood up swiftly and dramatically, causing the poor solicitor to shrink back in his chair like a frightened, beady-eyed mole.

"Those, too, have been left to Miss Cruella and cannot be touched, along with the capital," he said, his hands shaking.

She threw her glass, sending it crashing to the floor. Sir Huntley looked scandalized. I swear, if he had been able, he would have sunken into his chair and disappeared.

"If that is all," she said dismissively, "you may leave now, Sir Huntley." Mama was angry. Angrier than I had ever seen her. But the funny little man in the tweed suit didn't budge. He didn't take her cue to leave even when she stood up.

"I'm sorry, Lady De Vil, but I'm afraid there are conditions Miss Cruella needs to be made aware of before I leave," he said, looking rather uncomfortable at this unusual and unsightly show of emotion.

"Well then, as neither of you have need for me any longer, I will excuse myself," Mama said, storming out of the room. And then I was alone, facing a man who looked more like a bulldog in a tweed suit than a solicitor, when all I wanted to do was chase after my poor mama.

Sir Huntley shuffled his papers rather uncomfortably for a few more moments before breaking the silence. "I'm sure your mother is under tremendous stress," he said, trying to excuse her behavior. "Your father wanted to be clear about the conditions of his will. He wants you to keep the De Vil name, even after you marry. You are the last of the De Vil line. And since there is no male heir, it is up to you to keep the family name alive for future generations." I quickly agreed, eager to find my mama and console her, eager to tell her I was on her side, eager to see if she had forgiven me for all the terrible things that uppity nurse had said to her. But the bespectacled mole kept talking. "To be clear, Miss Cruella, should you marry and take your husband's name, the fortune will revert to your mother."

"I understand what keeping the family name means, Sir Huntley." The man narrowed his eyes at me.

"Your father was concerned you wouldn't be properly taken care of should the fortune revert to Lady De Vil," he said, shuffling his papers nervously again.

"I understand, Sir Huntley. I do. I don't plan to marry anyone. But if I do, for some reason, go mad and decide to marry, I promise to keep my father's name." The man cleared his throat again, clearly still nervous, indicating he had more to say.

"You say this now, Miss Cruella. But there may be a day when you meet someone who changes your mind." Sir Huntley was right, but neither of us knew it yet.

"It would take a remarkable man to change my mind, Sir Huntley. Someone who wanted the same things I want out of life. Someone willing to give me my independence, and be willing to take my father's name. Someone like my father. But I doubt I will ever meet such a man, and if I do, I assure you, sir, I will preserve my father's name. It's the least I can do for such a great man." Sir Huntley looked relieved, but still had no intention of letting me go after my mama to see if all was well between us. I desperately wanted to see her before she left for her trip.

"He also left a message, Miss Cruella. It's rather personal, but I trust you will understand its meaning." He cleared his throat, continuing. "He said to find someone worthy of you. He said he would rather have someone treat you like a treasure than give you treasures. Someone who shows you his love with his words, and his actions, not by buying you gifts."

"Thank you, Sir Huntley, I believe I understand," I said. I stood to signal it was time for him to leave. Sir Huntley was a man who understood social cues, and his job was done. At least for that day.

Sir Huntley and I said our goodbyes at the front door, and Jackson let him out. I was longing to go up and see my mother. But as I turned to make my way up the stairs, I met Anita coming down them. "Cruella, how are you? Let's go upstairs to your room. You must be exhausted. Would you like me to get you some tea?" Anita was always there for me. Always so sweet.

"Thank you, Anita. But I want to check on my mama."

By the door, Jackson cleared his throat. "Miss Cruella," he said, "your mother has already left for her trip. I know she was sorry she couldn't say good-bye herself." I was confused, but to say so would show I didn't know what was going on in my own household. I didn't want to betray my composure. But I think Jackson read the look of surprise on my face. He knew the rules. He acted as though I knew of my mother's plans even though I did not. "Her trip around the world, Miss. I'm sure she told you about it, and it's simply slipped your mind with the recent events. She said to let you know she would be back by the end of summer in time to see you off to boarding school."

"Yes, her trip, of course." My mind was reeling. She had been with me in the morning room just moments earlier. "But—her things—how did she pack so quickly?" I asked.

"Her trunks were already packed and waiting in the car," he said. *Already packed.* She must have packed them as soon as Papa died. And she hadn't told me. She'd just left without saying goodbye.

Anita took my hand gently in hers. And even though it felt like my world was falling apart, somehow, that gave me the strength to keep going.

I remember saying something to the effect of, "I see. Very well, Jackson. Miss Anita and I will take our lunch in the dining room today," or something of the like. I was the lady of the house, after all— that is at least until my mother returned home, and I needed to start acting like it.

## CHAPTER III

# DEARLY DEPARTED

Mama was off traveling for that entire summer before I went off to finishing school. She wrote only to make arrangements for the start of the school term, for me and Anita. Looking back now, I think she was angry with me because I was with Papa right before he died and she wasn't. I think that was the real reason behind her rage, not those lies that idiot nurse told her. I think she was hurt and disappointed she didn't have the opportunity to say goodbye. And I think she was hurt Papa had left me everything. I honestly didn't blame her. I would have done anything I could to mend our relationship again, but it was impossible to do so when she was away.

Thank goodness for Anita. Thank goodness she was going away with me to school, so I didn't have to go alone. I had never been to a real school before, only lessons with Miss Pricket in the schoolroom. Not that finishing school was *real* school. Not really. It was just to teach me how to be a lady, and I knew that already thanks to Mama's fastidious training. Of course there would be a series of subjects at our disposal, like literature, French, art, and so forth, but the main focus would be how to conduct ourselves properly at various social functions. At least that was my general understanding of things, as far as I gathered from the daughters of the women in my mother's social circle; they were sent there for a year or longer, depending on how long their mothers wanted them out of their hair before they were brought back home to be entered into society. Thank goodness Miss Pricket was on her way back home to me again. She would make everything clear and handle all the details.

Honestly, the idea of school and everything it was to prepare me for in life seemed a ghastly bore to me, so I couldn't have been happier that Anita was going to accompany me. In one of my letters to my mother, I had insisted that she make the suggestion to Anita's guardian. I remember the letter she sent back to me in reply. It was so dry and impersonal. But what bothered me even more was that she had sent no gifts while she was away. Not the entire time she was gone. It was so unlike her. That's how I knew she had stopped loving me. And I had no idea how I could make her happy again.

But I was young, and I was distracted by the prospect of going away to school with my best friend. Anita and I had decided we would make the most of it. The summer flew by in a flurry. The school provided us with a list of all the possessions I was expected to bring. School clothes were selected, trunks packed, and Mrs. Baddeley was planning to make preserves and other goodies to send along with me. Anita and I felt as if we were preparing for a grand adventure.

Anita fit right into life at my home. She was

practically living with me at that point. She stayed over almost every night. The staff loved her. She actually took an interest in Mrs. Baddeley's stories, and she impressed Miss Pricket with her incessant reading, and how quickly she was picking up French. And as for me, she had become more than just a best friend. She was my family. She didn't always go on about my mama the way Miss Pricket did, always assuring me of her love, but she comforted me in other ways. She calmed my fears about the future and stayed up to make me tea when I had a terrible dream about Papa. I wouldn't have survived that summer without her.

While we counted down the days of summer and waited for our real adventure to begin, we did all the things we thought we would have to give up once we were transformed into young ladies. Things only little girls were allowed to do. Every day we did something we had loved doing as children: we had tea parties with my dolls, snuck down to the kitchen and stole tarts while Mrs. Baddeley wasn't looking, and dressed like characters from our favorite stories and acted them out for Miss Pricket and the servants. But my favorite times during that summer were staying up late at night reading from the book of fairy tales my papa had given me. The night before we left for school, we stayed up well past our bedtime reading together and imagining our own fairy tales.

"I don't think we have to give up reading our fairy and adventure stories, Cruella," said Anita.

"I agree! I don't think I could ever give them up, even when I'm an old lady," I said. "My favorites are the Princess Tulip stories," I added dreamily, halfway between our world and the world in which Princess Tulip lived. "She's so brave and outspoken! She's not afraid of anything, or anyone, or to say what's on her mind."

"But she wasn't always that way," Anita pointed out. "Remember the story about her and the Beast Prince? She was very different then." Anita was right. She *had* been very different then, but that's what made Tulip so utterly amazing to me. She had started out a dim-witted princess and turned into this magnificently brave and brazen woman. Anita continued, "My favorite stories are after the Great War, when she helped Oberon and the Tree Lords." Her eyes widened. "The way she went to the Rock Giants all by herself and talked them into helping the Tree Lords in their fight with the Dark Fairy's dragon was so awe-inspiring."

"I know," I agreed, "that was amazing! But I felt sorry for the Dark Fairy. I can't believe those witches brought her back to life."

"Ah, let me guess, you're talking about Circe and Tulip again." It was Miss Pricket; she was standing in the doorway. "Cruella, I need you to finish picking out the things you want to take to school with you. Anita is already packed and her cases are downstairs. I would like to see yours down there before this night is through." As excited as I was about starting this adventure with Anita, I really was nervous about leaving home. I had just lost my father, and it seemed as though I might have lost my mother as well. I wanted to put off leaving as long as I could.

"Yes, Miss Pricket," I said in a singsong school-girl fashion. "I'm sorry we can't all be as perfect as Anita." Anita laughed.

"Oh, Cruella. I'm not perfect. I just can't wait to leave! I'm so excited," said Anita, blushing.

"I'm excited, too," I said. "But perhaps a little nervous." Anita put her hand on mine.

"Of course you're nervous. You're leaving home for the first time."

"How I will miss that sweet nature of yours, Anita," Miss Pricket said, smiling at both of us.

"Miss Pricket," I said, changing the subject. "Do you think the other girls will like us? What do you think they will be like?"

"I think they'll be very much like you and Miss Anita. Though perhaps not so interested in fairy tales, at least not the sort you two fancy, and not quite as smart or pretty, I would wager."

"Then they will be nothing like us," I said, laughing.

"Oh, Cruella stop," Anita chided gently. "I'm sure we will like the girls at school. This is our grand adventure, remember? Miss Pricket, you met the schoolmistress. What was she like?" Leave it to Anita to ask something sensible.

"She was a matronly woman. Very austere and serious. You'd better watch yourself around her, the pair of you!" Everything Miss Pricket said that evening sent us into peals of laughter. It was infectious, because soon Miss Pricket was laughing, too. It was because Anita was there. Anita could soften my sharp tongue, and she could charm Miss Pricket into laughing.

"What were the other girls like? Did you see any of them? Were they all terrible snobs?" I asked.

Miss Pricket just laughed. "You will have to see for yourself when you get there, Cruella. Now please finish selecting the things you would like me to pack for you or I am going to take Anita with me into the other room so you're not distracted. Don't forget, your mother is arriving early tomorrow morning to see you off to school."

"Yes, Miss Pricket, we promise to devote ourselves entirely to our tasks," I said, laughing, as she left the room. When she was gone, I turned to Anita. "I *am* curious about the other girls, Anita, aren't you? And the teachers. My goodness, I bet they're all a bunch of upstart in-betweens."

"What's an in-between?" Anita asked. My heart sank. I had been in such a jovial, lighthearted mood, I had forgotten myself. Anita didn't know about my nicknames.

"Well," I said slowly, "Miss Pricket is an in-between. She doesn't quite fit in downstairs with the servants, but she's not exactly accepted into the more elite social circles. She's somewhere . . . in between." I saw the hurt and realization wash over Anita's face.

"Like me," she said.

"No, Anita! You're different from the other in-betweens, you're better! " I said, trying to make her understand.

"But you love Miss Pricket, don't you, even though she's, as you say, an in-between?"

I thought about it. "I suppose I do, in my own way. But not the way I love you. You're different, Anita. Miss Pricket is my servant. You're my friend.

You are my *best* friend, and therefore associated with the finest of social circles. No one at school will look down on you, even the snootiest of girls won't dare."

"You know I don't care about such things, Cruella. I don't care what those girls think of me."

"Well," I said with a smile, "I will make sure they think nothing but the best of you, Anita. You're much more than an in-between." I got up, remembering something I wanted to bring with me, and went to my jewelry box to fish them out.

"What's that?" Anita asked as I took the small box from the jewelry case.

"Antique earrings my father gave me. What do you think of them?" I asked, trying them on. "Do they look too much like old lady earrings? Or will I fit right in with all the snots at finishing school?"

"Oh, I think they're beautiful. And your father gave them to you. You should wear them, Cruella, you really should," she said, handing the box back to me and looking sad. Dear, sweet Anita. Always so loving, so caring and sentimental. "You know I almost wore them to Papa's funeral. I had honestly almost forgotten about them until that day, but I couldn't bring myself to put them on."

"Why, Cruella?"

"I don't know, I had the strangest feeling while I was holding them. An odd feeling of foreboding, like I would never be happy again. And then I remembered my papa's story about the earrings. That they were cursed." A chill ran down my neck, and the fine hair on my arm stood on end. Anita swallowed, nervous.

"You don't *really* believe they're cursed, do you? I'm sure you were just sad about your father passing away. I think you should bring them with you and wear them at school. It will be a lovely way to remember him." Anita was so sweet that I felt the chill vanish, and the room was filled with warmth again.

"You're right. I'm being silly. I'm going to put them on right now." But when I brought them to my ears, it happened again. That feeling of doom. I couldn't shake it.

"Cruella, are you okay?" Anita asked. I couldn't answer. I didn't know. Perhaps it was nerves. Everything in my life was on the verge of changing.

"Are you nervous about leaving home? Nervous about seeing your mother tomorrow?" Anita asked. I honestly couldn't say. But the strange feeling stayed with me for the rest of the evening. It invaded my sleep, filling my dreams with pirates, otherworldly magical lands, and a dark forest filled with glowing candles.

✤ ✤ ✤ ✤

By the next morning my trunks were packed, and they were sitting beside Anita's and Miss Pricket's, piled high in the entryway at the foot of the grand staircase. I was so happy that Anita would be traveling with me to school, and Miss Pricket was to accompany us for the entire journey to see us settled. She would stay for a fortnight before returning back to London.

All of us were antsy as we waited for my mother to arrive. "We will have to leave soon, Miss Cruella. We don't want to miss our train," Miss Pricket said, as if I wasn't already aware. I certainly wouldn't miss her flair for stating the obvious. Jackson cleared his throat and tapped on the glass face of his pocket watch to say he agreed. I was honestly rather anxious to see my mother, and all of Miss Pricket's and Jackson's fidgeting was driving me mad. I turned to Anita.

"Anita, how do I look?" She smiled, and some of my nerves melted.

"You look beautiful, Cruella, as always." I wanted to look perfect for Mama. I had put on one of my best traveling dresses in her favorite color, dusty rose, and wore the jade earrings Papa had given me. I couldn't believe I was going to see her after all this time. And right before I had to leave for school.

"Oh, I see a car now. That must be her," Jackson said, going out to greet my mother. But when he returned, she wasn't with him. Instead, a legion of footmen trailed behind him, all carrying boxes. The footmen piled the boxes on the round table in the center of the entryway, crowding the vase of flowers that sat in its usual place. Jackson motioned to one of the maids standing nearby to help the footmen with the boxes that threatened to topple over. "Paulie, help the footman with those packages if you will?" I blinked. And in that moment, I knew. She wasn't coming.

"Miss Cruella, these packages all have your name on them," Paulie said. "I will pack them up for you and have them sent along so you can open them at school. But it seems your mother was eager for you to take this one along on your journey," she said, handing me a rather large white box with a red bow. Paulie steadied the box while I removed the lid, exposing the most magnificent fur coat I had ever seen. It was long and white with a black collar, just like the one she had given me when I was a little girl, but somehow even more lovely. In the box was a small square note card that simply read:

*Distinguish yourself.*

"Oh, Cruella, it's lovely," said Anita, with no hint of jealousy or sadness like Miss Pricket usually displayed.

"Miss Cruella," Miss Pricket said, in a tone

that, for the first time, was obvious in its disdain for my mother. "You won't need that at school. Let's leave it here where it will be safe." I rarely pulled rank with Miss Pricket—she was, after all, my governess, and I was in her charge—not to mention, I trusted her. But something in me shifted quite suddenly, and I heard my voice snap: "My mother would like me to take it along, and I am going to take it."

"Miss Cruella, none of the other girls will bring along such fine things," she said, more gently this time, but it was too late. I had heard her scorn. I knew how she felt about Mama. And I knew she was wrong.

I simply handed her the note Mama had included in the box, reminding her of what it said. "My mama says I'm to distinguish myself," I said as Jackson helped me on with my coat. "And I plan to, with style!" I walked out the door, ready to embark on our grand excursion. I felt brave and proud. I was distinguishing myself. Just like my mother.

## CHAPTER IV

# LADIES OF ACCOMPLISHMENT

At first school was everything Anita and I wanted it to be. Our academy was a converted mansion, brick covered with ivy, you know the sort. It had that awe-inspiring architecture one expects to find nestled away in the country, surrounded by rolling hills, groves of trees, and a lavish park on the school grounds. It was really quite beautiful.

Anita, of course, gravitated to subjects like poetry, classic literature, and mythology, while I enjoyed learning about social ranks and the titles that went along with them. Both of us loved our classes in music and painting, but I detested French lessons, while Anita seemed to enjoy them, having proven herself quite good at them in my schoolroom back home. But what we both loved most were our daily walks around the grounds through the park. It was our time to talk about our day, to gossip about the other girls and our instructors.

Anita genuinely liked being outdoors. She could sit for hours just looking at the trees, or the leaves floating down the creek we happened upon on one of our walks. And she loved watching the birds and squirrels. I honestly couldn't give a damn about nature; I just liked getting away from everyone. I couldn't stand being locked up with all those simpering, foolish girls, talking of nothing but when they would be entered into society and eventually married. That seemed to be their singular focus: finding the richest, most well-connected man and marrying him.

Within the first few days of my arrival, I realized young women in my social circle went to school not to better themselves, not to learn something of the world, not to have an adventure—but to find a husband. Or at least that was the objective of all the young women Anita and I went to school with. It was likely they would snare husbands right after they were entered into society, and I supposed their education would teach them enough that they could have intelligent conversations in their drawing rooms with their guests. But they would never be permitted to sit with the men after dinner and have the *real* conversations. The real conversations were reserved for the men. They got to talk about what was going on in the world, the places they traveled, and the books they'd read. We ladies got to speak of the weather and which fork went where in a dinner setting. The more time I spent at Miss Upturn's Academy for Young Ladies, the more I realized it was absolutely bursting with simpleminded girls who were all relentlessly mercenary in the pursuit of their happily ever after.

I became even more convinced that this wasn't the life for me.

It wasn't the life I wanted. I wanted something more. I wanted freedom. I didn't want to be tied down to a household or a husband. I wanted to do what I pleased, whenever I wanted. And I didn't see that happening with a husband. Not unless I found someone truly unique and remarkable, like my papa. And I doubted that would ever happen. Besides, unlike many of the girls I went to school with, I didn't need to marry. I had my father's money. I had the De Vil name. And I had the most engaging companion I could ever want in Anita.

Despite my unconventional ideas about my future and how much I detested the other students, I really did love every moment of my education. We were to be made into accomplished ladies. We were taught how to direct a conversation at dinner: how to steer it in another direction if the talk became unsuitable or awkward, how to avoid speaking directly on any subject that was of a personal or sensitive nature, and most important, the virtues of speaking indirectly while making our point clear. I may not have wanted to get married, but I did want to learn how to conduct myself with decorum. I wanted to make my mama proud. And about half-way through our first semester, I learned I was going to have the opportunity. My mama was coming to visit me that day for my birthday. I hadn't seen her since my father died.

"Anita, I'm a little nervous about seeing my mama." It was Saturday, and we were sitting in the garden, taking advantage of a rare sunny afternoon. We had spread out a blanket, and Anita had arranged some little sandwiches and cakes for us to enjoy in the sunshine. Her little birthday gift to me.

"What are you two going to do later? When is she arriving?" she asked.

"She's taking me out for dinner. We're going to the Criterion!" I said. Anita's eyes got wide. "I know. It's quite fancy! I'm going to wear my best dress. I can't wait to see her." Suddenly, Anita's face reminded me of how Miss Pricket's would sometimes look when I talked about my mother.

"What's wrong, Anita? I can see if you can come along, if you like, so you don't have to spend the evening alone." Anita wrapped her shawl around her shoulders.

"No, Cruella. You should have some time with

your mother on your own. You haven't seen her in ages. It will do you both some good to spend some time together."

"Well, how are you going to spend your evening?" I asked. I hated the idea of Anita spending the evening alone, or worse, what if one of those snotty twits gave her trouble without me there to protect her?

"Doing homework, reading. The usual," she said, picking little white flowers and linking them together by their stems. "Maybe I'll catch up with Princess Tulip, see how she's doing."

"Don't read too far along without me!" I said. "If you do, you will have to catch me up."

"Cruella, we've read all these stories hundreds of times, I won't need to catch you up!" She put the string of flowers on my head like a crown.

"There, now you look like a princess," she said, smiling. "You're going to have a lovely night with your mama."

Later that night, she helped me get ready. I must have tried on every single dress I owned. "Don't forget your fur, Cruella. Your mother would love to see you in it, I'm sure." She handed it to me. I was so nervous. I hadn't seen my mama in so long, and she had been so upset with me. I feared she believed what that horrible nurse had said: that I was the reason Papa died. But I pushed all that out of my mind as I kissed Anita on the cheek and went down to wait for the car. But Mama wasn't waiting for me. It was Miss Pricket, saddled with a bundle of packages and a hamper full of food. I saw that customary sad look she often wore on her face.

I ended up spending my seventeenth birthday with Miss Pricket and Anita in our room, reading well into the night and eating the delicious food Mrs. Baddeley had sent along. It was a lovely evening. I was with two of my favorite people, and I knew my mother loved me. She had, after all, sent me some beautiful gifts.

☙ ☙ ☙ ☙

Though you wouldn't have known it by looking at her, Anita was really out of place in Miss Upturn's Academy for Young Ladies. She flourished in her academic pursuits but found all of my favorite subjects foolish. She had no use whatsoever for the more "frivolous" subjects, as she called them. But my goodness, Anita was such a smart little thing. Quiet but not mousy, smart but never condescending. She was sweet, observant, studious, and always conducted herself like a proper young lady. And without me there to protect her, those girls would have eaten her alive!

Thankfully, we spent almost all our time together. We had a room to ourselves; my mama had arranged it. Most of the other girls had to share four to a room, but my family had given the school large endowments, which meant Anita and I were rewarded with more privacy. The room had a lovely view of the gardens; one of the walls was almost entirely windows. The quarters were large enough for two canopied beds, two wardrobes, and two vanities, and had a cozy little sitting area where we shared our morning tea together and chatted before we went down to have breakfast with the other girls. Even though, in the first few weeks, I didn't like most of the girls at school, I did hope I would turn out to be wrong about them. I was hoping we'd find at least one other girl like Anita and myself who we could bring into our little circle. I decided to start a reading club. A few weeks into the school year I sprang my brilliant idea on Anita.

"What do you think, Anita? It might be a good way for us to get to know some of the other girls," I said to her one morning while we were getting ready to go down to breakfast. Anita didn't look convinced.

"I thought you hated all the other girls, Cruella. Aren't they all spoiled daughters of your mother's friends?" It was true, most of them were. And I had known some of them since I was young, but I didn't know them *really*. Not the way I knew Anita. At most, we had shared occasional polite conversations at various functions.

However, there was one girl I knew well. Arabella. She was my mother's best friend's daughter. I had never really cared for her and had done my best to shield Anita from her since we'd arrived at school. If she got one whiff of Anita's background we would never hear the end of it. So I was thankful Anita would sometimes come off a little standoffish with people she didn't know. It honestly made her seem like most of the entitled girls at school. But really, she was just shy and rather focused on her studies.

"I don't know, maybe we'll find someone who loves the same books as us," I said. "I'll make a posting for our club and put it up on the bulletin board."

Anita sighed. "Okay, I suppose. Let's see what happens." We went down to breakfast together and found our little corner of the room where we usually sat, away from Arabella and her haughty friends. I was working on my posting for the bulletin board and Anita was reading a book we had been assigned when a snotty voice said, "Good morning, Cruella. And who is this? I haven't met your friend." I looked up, and my stomach knotted when I saw that it was Arabella.

"Good morning, Arabella. This is my friend Anita." Anita looked up from her book.

Arabella still wore her hair in ringlets, like she was a little girl. Long blond ringlets that fell softly around her pale face. She looked like a precious doll with her perfect porcelain skin, and her shining blue eyes that looked as if they might have been made of glass. But really, she was a monstrous girl in the guise of an angel.

Arabella was the youngest of one of my mother's dearest friends. We had been thrust together since childhood, and I wasn't happy when I found myself forced into her company again once I got to school. My mother had given up years before in trying to make us the best of friends as she and her dear friend Lady Slaptton so desperately wanted. It was clear from early childhood that Arabella and I had nothing in common, much like me and the rest of my mother's friends' children. And Arabella really was the worst kind of girl.

"Oh yes, I remember Anita from back home. Your little pet." She smirked. "What are you working on there, Cruella?" she asked, looking at the posting I was drafting.

"I'm creating a reading club," I said. Arabella laughed under her breath. "Still reading those silly fairy tales you always talked about when we were young? What was that princess's name again? Something stupid. Oh yes, Tulip. Have you ever heard of a Princess Tulip? I never have. Then again, I've never heard of anyone named Cruella. So what do I know?"

"Yes, I still love those stories," I said. "And so does Anita." Arabella sniggered again. "Well then, you're a perfect match. But I don't think you will find anyone interested in your fairy-tale club. The last thing any of us want to do with our spare time is read more books. You know it ruins your eyes, Anita. You're going to look old before your time if you keep reading like that."

"I don't think that's true, Arabella," Anita said, going right back to her book. I could see Arabella's wheels turning. She was trying to think of something clever to say, but I deflected her.

"I'm sorry, Arabella, Anita wants to be prepared for Miss Babble's class right after breakfast."

Arabella huffed. "Well, I won't bother you any further then." Her curls spun as she turned on her heels to leave. "See you in class!" she called, her hair swaying and bouncing as she walked away. I swear that girl purposely walked that way to make her hair sway, superficial fool that she was.

"Well, that was a good start. We're making new friends already," I said. Anita didn't even really seem to notice. I knew she wasn't interested in making new friends, and she was only humoring my idea that we might find a treasure of a girl hidden among all those fools and idiots. Anita was determined to make the best of the education her guardian was providing for her. That was more than I could say for most of the other young ladies attending our classes.

After breakfast, we went to Miss Babble's class to discuss the book Anita had been so diligently reading during breakfast. It was a Jane Austen story. I can't recall which one now, but I do remember Anita seemed to be the only person in class who truly grasped the author's intentions. Miss Babble was always reluctant to call on Anita because she was usually the only person who raised her hand. "Yes, well, if there is no one else . . . Miss Anita, will you share your thoughts?"

"Miss Austen makes astute observations about the social classes with her various works, never mind how keenly she brings the marginalization of women to the front of most of her stories, most especially young women with few or no prospects."

I can still see the looks on the other students' unblinking faces. Like little rabbits being stared down by a wolf.

The wolf, of course, was Arabella Slaptton, the beast from breakfast. She was cleverer than all the other girls, so she was their ringleader. She always had a sharp word or pointed look to contribute when Anita would speak up in class. Arabella from this point forward would never miss the opportunity to make Anita look bad.

"Well, you would know all about young women with few to no prospects, wouldn't you, Anita?" said Arabella. I jumped up from my seat immediately.

"What do you know? Who told you that?" I asked. Arabella laughed.

"Oh, everyone knows, Cruella. But I thought I would see for myself, and clearly Anita is not only lacking in a proper background, but she is also lacking in social graces."

"You take that back, Arabella Slaptton. Take it back right now or I will show you the meaning of your name!" Arabella smirked at me like I had just given her a gift. And I suppose I had.

"Miss Babble, did you hear what Cruella just said? She threatened me! What do you intend to do about it?"

"Yes, Miss Babble, what do you intend to do about it?" I said mockingly.

"I intend to send you to the headmistress, Miss Cruella. Leave at once!"

I was shocked. "You can't be serious." But Miss Babble wasn't budging.

"Oh, I assure you, I am entirely serious. A lady doesn't threaten other students." Her cheeks and neck had turned red from being flustered. She suddenly reminded me of Mrs. Baddeley, which made me laugh. "What, may I ask, is so funny, young lady?" she asked, making me laugh harder.

"I just can't believe you're actually going to let Arabella get away with insulting Anita, and send me to the headmistress for defending her!" I was so angry, but I didn't want to give Arabella the benefit of showing my emotions. So I kept laughing it off.

"I hardly see what was so insulting by stating the truth, Miss Cruella. Now please leave my classroom at once." Miss Babble's face was getting more scarlet by the minute, and I fear I lost all sense of composure in that moment.

"Stating the truth? How dare you insult Anita like that, you haughty, jumped-up little—"

"Cruella. Cruella, please." It was Anita. She had gotten up from her seat and put her hand on my shoulder. It was always Anita who saved me from myself. "Cruella, please stop. I'm fine. Let's go take a walk."

"Yes, might I suggest you *both* take a walk,

directly to the headmistress's office," said Miss Babble.

But of course we never made it there, at least not on that occasion. I was too angry, and my ears were ringing with the laughter of those simple fools as we left the classroom.

"Who do they think they are, laughing at you like that?" I huffed, not giving Anita time to reply. "And saying that about your prospects. What does it matter if it's true? She had no right to expose you in class like that."

"I'm not ashamed of my background, Cruella. But maybe you are. Are you sure you're not upset because I'm an embarrassment to you?" I stopped dead in my tracks, looked her straight in the eye, and grabbed her hands in mine.

"No! Don't be an idiot, Anita, of course not. You're my friend. If anyone is an embarrassment it's that twit Arabella. You can see why we never became friends."

Anita laughed. "Oh, I remember her," she said. "She was always horrible, even as a little girl.

I wonder if she isn't hurt that you're no longer friends."

"I bet she's jealous of you," I said. "Why else would she make such a point of trying to make you look bad?"

Anita's smiled faded. "Because that's how everyone in this school feels, even the teachers. I see it on all their faces, even the nice teachers. The ones who aren't looking down their noses at me are giving me sad looks. They know I'm only here because of you."

It quickly became clear that word of Anita's lack of background had been circulating. And even though she was kind to everyone, it wasn't long before she was snubbed by most of the other girls and even some of the instructors. And I didn't make any friends defending her.

It was safe to say we were the least popular girls at school. Not that I minded, really. I didn't care for a single girl in the entirety of our class. And the staff and headmistress? I didn't give a jot for any of them, either.

I mean, what were the headmistress and the

teachers if they weren't glorified servants? Oh, they might have come from respectable enough families or the same circumstances as Anita, making them in-betweens, but really, who were they to cast judgment on Anita? It became a daily battle, and I found myself spending more time in the headmistress's office than in class. And really, she wasn't any help. She was just as insufferable as our nasty classmates and most of the instructors.

I laugh to myself now, remembering a particular day when I received a summons to the headmistress's office. I was in Miss Babble's class when the note arrived asking me to come to the office. All the girls in class looked very pleased with themselves. I don't think they could have been more pleased if they'd all received proposals from the richest men alive, so I knew they were up to something.

"Miss Babble, what is this about?" I asked.

"I suggest you go to the headmistress's office and find out, Miss Cruella," she said with a smug look on her face. Ever since that scene with Arabella, things in Miss Babble's class had been wretched.

Those fools took every opportunity to say something wicked about Anita, and Miss Babble did nothing to stop them.

Well, if it was a battle they wanted, I was prepared.

I decided to make a detour before heading to her office. In a quick pit stop at my room, I put on my jade earrings and fur coat. You know the ones of which I speak. I wanted to look the part if I was going to give the headmistress a piece of my mind. I wanted to look fabulous and imposing, like Mama did when she was ticking someone off.

"Here to see Miss Upturn again, Miss Cruella?" asked the frumpy-looking woman sitting at the desk right outside the headmistress's office. Yes, that was our headmistress's name: Miss Upturn. I think she thought it was a posh name, but to me it sounded common. And it seemed all too fitting, what with all the times she'd turned her nose up at Anita on the occasions we had been sent to her office.

Miss Frumpypants let me into Miss Upturn's office. The headmistress was sitting at her desk, dressed in a plain but stately brown dress suit, and had what looked to be a dead quail on her head, the feathers going every which way.

It was a very unfortunate hat.

And to make matters worse, it was very out of date. Much like her dress. She made pretense at being busy when her assistant led me into her office and directed me to stand near the chair across from her desk. Miss Upturn kept me standing there while her beady little eyes darted around her desk, like a deranged bird looking for something to do. She didn't even bother to look at me for several minutes. I could tell she was putting off speaking with me as long as she could.

Simple woman. Barely an in-between. *Finally*, she looked up at me.

"Miss Cruella. It has been brought to my attention that you are causing quite the disturbance in Miss Babble's class," she said, looking at me with her too small, too round eyes. She really was a startling sight.

"Yes, Miss Upturn. The other students have

been horrible to Anita and Miss Babble does nothing about it. And she refuses to call on Anita in class. I don't understand why she insists on ignoring her. She is the only student in our class who actually has something of value to share, and who has taken the time to actually read her assignments," I said. The quail wobbled on Miss Upturn's head as she sighed. It would have made me laugh if I hadn't seen the look of disgust on her face when I mentioned Anita's name. This made me dislike the woman even more.

"Honestly, Cruella, I don't understand your fascination with that girl. You have been to this office countless times, all on account of her. She is beneath you in every way. I frankly don't understand what you see in her. An education here will only take Anita so far. Do you understand what I'm telling you? I'm sure you two were very close in childhood, and it's wonderful to have such friends when you're young. But it's time you understand you will both be in very different social circles once you are entered in society. You will eventually go your own ways, and I'd hate to see you discount and alienate the girls who share your social standing, because those are the young ladies you will be spending time with in social situations, not Anita."

"Anita is my best friend, and a very good friend of my family's. I would hate my mother to find out how poorly she is being treated by you and your staff, not to mention how you let the students mock her. I'm not sure how everyone found out about Anita's lack of circumstances, but that should have no bearing on her getting the education her guardians are paying for her to receive."

"Well, Miss Cruella, it was your mother who informed me of Anita's circumstances, and while she indulges your friendship to a point, she wanted Anita to be reminded of her place. Your family has been so generous in their endowments to our school, Miss Cruella, I thought the least I could do was honor your mother's request."

I was shocked. But I didn't blink. "While I am aware of my mother's concerns, Miss Upturn, I would suggest that you speak with your staff and make it clear that Miss Anita is to be treated with respect, or I will personally see to it that this school no longer receives those endowments."

Miss Upturn laughed under her breath, making the bird on her hat wobble again. It was all I could do not to burst out laughing. Clearly she didn't realize my situation. And taking a page out of my mother's book, I took control of the conversation before she could elaborate on her laugher.

"This school is ridiculous! *Honestly.* The idea of inferiors like you and your staff instructing *me* how to conduct myself in social circles that quite frankly would never permit you makes me laugh. How dare you look down your noses at Anita! All it will take is one phone call to my solicitor and the endowments will cease!" I took Sir Huntley's calling card out of my handbag and placed it on her desk. "You may, of course, confirm all of this with Sir Huntley if you wish. Now if you will excuse me, Miss Upturn, I have some letters to write and calls to make before I start packing for winter break." Miss Upturn sat there dumbfounded. *Gobsmacked* is a better word.

She was speechless, staring at the card, while the bird on her head stood stock-still, staring at me. I had achieved my purpose. I only wished I'd had the courage to do it sooner. I felt so powerful in that moment, wearing the earrings my papa had given me and the lovely coat Mama insisted I take along with me to school. I understood in that moment that I got my power from looking my best. Just like my mama.

I couldn't wait to tell Anita all about it. I turned to walk out of the room, but Miss Upturn's voice stopped me. "I'm sorry for any misunderstanding, Miss Cruella. Of course I will see that the staff treats Miss Anita with more respect. You can be assured of that." I didn't bother turning around when I answered. I simply said, "See that you do!"

"So you won't be making that call to your solicitor then, Miss Cruella?" she asked, her voice sounding very small and not at all like her usual imposing self.

I glanced back over my shoulder and added, "No, Miss Upturn, not while Anita is treated with respect, I don't expect I will have to." And then I smiled at the woman, taking delight in twisting the screw a little further. "Oh, and, Miss Upturn . . . I'll see that my solicitor includes a little something extra for you with our next endowment. Might I suggest you use it to buy yourself a new hat!" Then I swished my fur coat around me, as I had seen my mother do countless times, and I dramatically exited the office. I was magnificent.

I'm not embarrassed to say I was very proud of myself that day. I not only stood up for my best friend, but I devised a way to make sure she would be treated fairly from that point forward. Of course, Miss Upturn turned out to be right in the end. I was young, and I let my childhood love blind me. I didn't see Anita back then as I do now.

Anita and I sat in our room and laughed together when I told her about my talk with Miss Upturn.

"Oh, Anita! You should have seen the look on her face! She was trembling in fear and anger. I thought that hat was going to fall right off her head!"

"But you didn't really tell her to get a new hat,

did you?" asked Anita, scandalized but laughing despite her sweet nature.

"I did! Isn't it a blast?" We both laughed so hard we annoyed the girls in the room next to us, but I didn't care. They were all horrid creatures. None of them had the sort of money my family did. Who were they to turn their noses up at Anita and me? If anyone was going to be looking down on anyone, it was going to be me looking down on them.

CHAPTER V

# HOME FOR THE
# HOLIDAYS

The Christmas holiday came upon us quickly, and I was so excited to spend it with Anita. I was even looking forward to seeing Miss Pricket, who said I could bring Anita home with me for the holidays since her guardians would be traveling out of the country. I didn't want her home alone with no one but servants to keep her company. I was so happy when Miss Pricket wrote to say I should bring Anita along, and that my mother wouldn't mind.

My mother was still traveling, but she continued to send me gifts, and sometimes she'd include a little something for Anita because she knew it would make me happy. I hoped she would be returning in time for the holidays. There was no indication that what Miss Upturn had said about my mama wanting her to keep Anita in her place was remotely true, so I had decided the woman was lying or had misunderstood something Mama had said. Leave it to a haughty in-between to take it upon herself to decide what my mother might or might not have wanted. Horrible woman.

Miss Pricket took the train to meet us at school so she could escort us back to London—first class, of course. We didn't travel any other way. She was full of the usual questions on the train back to London, asking about our studies, the other girls, our instructors. I didn't share my conversation with Miss Upturn, but we did tell her about all the things we had learned and how excited we were to start dance classes after the winter break. They were going to teach us how to dance properly for the upcoming season of balls and other social events. Even though neither of us were particularly interested in attending stupid balls, we did fancy the idea of learning how to dance. After all, every lady needed to know how to dance, even if it wasn't going to be at a stuffy ball or one's wedding day. I imagined Anita and myself dancing in exotic locations. And I fancied one day we would have a true adventure, but my grand ideas for the future were still forming and I wasn't ready to share them yet.

While I mused about that, Miss Pricket and Anita began chatting in French, and my daydreams turned to Christmas. I was so excited to help the servants trim the tree, and to see what Mrs. Baddeley was going to cook for our Christmas feast. But what I looked forward to most was seeing my mama. I desperately wanted to hear about her adventures. And I was so happy I would be spending the Christmas holiday with the two people I loved most in the world: Mama and Anita. I wanted so desperately to mend things with Mama. To put all that nonsense with Papa's nurse and Papa's will behind us. I was so hoping that Christmastime would lend its magic to help us become friends again.

"I'm so happy you both seem to be enjoying

school," said Miss Pricket, bringing me out of my daydreams. I looked around our train compartment, almost surprised to find myself there. In my mind, I was already home with my mama. "Miss Cruella, I wanted to mention something before we got back to Belgrave Square." My stomach dropped. I thought for sure she was going to tell me my mama wouldn't be home for the holidays. "Your headmistress, Miss Upturn, called to tell me about your last conversation." But before I could say anything, Anita spoke up.

"It's not her fault, Miss Pricket, it's mine. . . ." Miss Pricket took Anita's hand.

"Don't be a goose, Anita. Neither of you are at fault," she said, turning her attention to me. "I'm just so proud of you, Miss Cruella, for standing up to your teachers and headmistress like that." I was so relieved. I had been sure she was going to take me to task. The very last thing I expected was Miss Pricket, of all people, commending me for threatening my headmistress.

"I can't wait to tell Mama," I said, laughing.

"She will be so proud of me." Miss Pricket was silent. "What is it?" I asked.

"I don't think we should share this with your mother, not just yet. Let's wait until after the holidays. I would hate to have anything ruin your time together." Miss Pricket looked uncomfortable.

"What aren't you telling me, Miss Pricket?"

She shook her head. "Let's speak of it later. Look, we're almost at the station."

But I insisted. Clearly I hadn't been paying attention to my lessons in taking social cues, putting poor Anita and Miss Pricket in an awkward situation.

"Cruella," Anita said, "I think what Miss Pricket is trying to say is that your mother wouldn't approve. You know she's never quite accepted our friendship." I didn't know what to say. Miss Pricket clapped her hands, snapping us out of the heavy mood that had fallen over our train compartment.

"Never mind that, girls. Let's not speak of it again. We're going to have an amazing winter break," she said. "Look, we're almost there." And before we knew it we were back in London. Dirty and cold as it was, I was happy to be back. I bundled myself in my fur coat against the chill and against the unsightly views of the less fashionable parts of the city until we were finally in Belgrave Square.

Home.

As our chauffeur helped us out of the car, it took everything within me not to dash through the front door to see Mama. The whole household was standing in attendance, waiting for us in the vestibule at the bottom of the grand staircase. I had forgotten how much I loved that beautiful room, with its giant crystal chandelier hanging above the round table that always had flowers upon it. Everyone was there except Mrs. Baddeley. No doubt busily preparing our holiday meal down in the dungeon. Funny, isn't it, how cooks, and head housekeepers for that matter, use the prefix Mrs. when they're not married? I wondered if it made them feel as though they were married to their jobs. And in a way I suppose they were. But if anyone was married to their job it was Jackson. *Mr.* Jackson, as the ghosts downstairs

111

called him. We didn't need a head housekeeper, not with Jackson around. Jackson, along with Mrs. Baddeley, took care of everything according to my mother's instruction. And would one day according to *my* instruction, when the house became mine.

I had decided after my father died that I wanted to be an independent woman. Never to marry. I took my father's final wishes to heart: I would keep his name. And there was no man worth his salt who would agree to take on his wife's name, unless of course she was the Queen of England, and though my family may have been grand and royally connected, I wasn't the Queen. But I thought I might like to emulate one. I thought of Queen Elizabeth I and how she never married. And look what she accomplished! I always felt I was destined for greatness. And look at me now. More fabulous than ever. Like a queen.

I imagined a happy unmarried life in that house with Anita. She likely wouldn't marry, either, given her prospects. I imagined she would be my companion, and we would travel the world together, stopping back at Belgrave Place to briefly refresh ourselves before taking off on our next adventure. I imagined us in places like Egypt, Paris, and Istanbul, wearing the local fashions, trying exotic foods, and sending postcards back home with lurid descriptions of our exploits.

I was excited to make my way to the morning room to see if Mama was there, when a woman I had never seen before broke off from the other ghosts and approached me. She was a tall, imposing woman with shocking white hair pulled into a severe bun. Her lips were perpetually pinched, as if she smelled something foul in the air. Her fingers were long and spindly and reminded me of spider's legs. She wore all black and had a large ring of keys hanging from her belt. She looked like an austere undertaker hoarding the keys to the underworld. I didn't like her on sight. She looked to Jackson to make the introductions.

"Welcome home," said Jackson. "We are so happy to have you and Miss Anita home for the holidays. Please let me introduce Mrs. Web. She is our new head housekeeper." From that moment on I would refer to her, at least in my mind, as the Spider. "Lady De Vil thought we needed a new head of household, as she is so often away," said Jackson. I said nothing. I just looked at the Spider in amazement, wondering why on earth she was there.

"She's not away *that* often," I said, eyeing the morning room and wanting to ask Mama what this was all about.

Miss Pricket tutted at me under her breath before addressing the Spider. "Excuse us, Mrs. Web, we have had a long journey. I am sure Miss Cruella and Miss Anita are eager to refresh themselves before dinner with Lady De Vil." She gave me a scolding look.

"Lady De Vil won't be here for dinner. She hasn't arrived home yet," said the Spider. "I'm sure she will make her way back to you as soon as she can," she added, seeming to take delight in my disappointment. Or maybe I had just imagined it. Either way, I felt my blood boiling. "In the meantime, if there is anything you need, please ring for me, Miss Cruella.

Your mother has directed me to act in her place while she is away."

I wanted to scream. How dare this woman think she could act in my mother's place? And where *was* my mother? I had been so looking forward to seeing her. I hadn't seen her the entire time I was away at school. Not once. And she rarely wrote me. Most of her news I learned from Miss Pricket, who was in constant correspondence. I had to do something to win back her favor.

"When will she be back?" I asked.

"Before Christmas, I'm sure," said Miss Pricket. Then she added quickly, "Come, girls. Let's get you settled in your rooms and unpacked. You've had a long journey." And she escorted Anita and me upstairs to our rooms. I remember looking down on all the servants as I reached the first landing. They seemed like ghosts to me, disappearing through the door under the stairs, but the most disturbing sight was Mrs. Web skittering behind them like a spider made of smoke and sulfur. I didn't like her one bit.

My room was exactly as I remembered it, and they had set Anita up in the rose room right across the hall from mine, the room I had come to think of as hers. "Miss Anita, your bags are in your usual room across the hall if you'd like to get settled," Miss Pricket said briskly. "I will be there in a few moments to help you unpack after I've helped Miss Cruella."

Anita smiled. "Thank you, Miss Pricket," she said, going off to the rose room.

"Miss Pricket, how would you feel about being my lady's maid? Of course, I would have to speak with Mama when she gets home, but I wanted to hear what you might think before I do." I was so hoping Miss Pricket would agree. She had been with me since I was quite young, and even though I found myself annoyed with her at times, I couldn't imagine a life without her. It made sense to me to ask her to be my lady's maid; it was a natural transition. Who else would I trust but my old governess for such an intimate position?

"Well, Miss Cruella, your mother did mention that you are too old for a governess, and asked if I would like to stay on as a lady's maid and companion," she said, smiling. "I was so hoping the news would please you."

"Oh yes, of course it does. I am so happy the idea agrees with *you*. Though I don't think I could bring myself to call you just Pricket . . . I have been calling you Miss Pricket for so long."

Miss Pricket laughed. "You may call me whatever you wish, Miss Cruella," she said, smiling at me.

"Speaking of new positions in the household, I was curious what you could tell me about Mrs. Web. Is she settling in?" I asked.

"Oh, she's settling in well enough." Miss Pricket was being her usual discreet self. She would never say a bad word about anyone. Well, that wouldn't do. If Miss Pricket was going to be my lady's maid, then she was going to have to act like one. And that meant giving me all the gossip from downstairs. So I prodded her a little, making it clear I didn't care for the woman, hoping Miss Pricket would open up to me.

"I just don't see why we need her. We were doing perfectly fine before. I wonder if Jackson and Mrs. Baddeley resent her presence. I know I do, the odious spider that she is."

"Oh, Miss Cruella. Don't speak about her like that." Miss Pricket wasn't taking the bait. I walked over to my vanity, sat down, and put on my jade earrings while I watched the woman who had cared for me my entire life unpack my trunks. I felt a tingling thrill at putting on the earrings. I felt more like a powerful lady when I wore them. And I realized in that moment my relationship with Miss Pricket had shifted. I was no longer her charge, but she still acted as though I was. It was an adjustment to be made in small steps, and I was about to take the first step. "Miss Pricket, if you're going to be my lady's maid then I expect to hear all the gossip. Mama tells me she hears about everything that goes on downstairs from Mrs. Smart, *her* lady's maid."

"Oh, I don't know, Miss Cruella." She pulled a

freshly pressed dress from my closet. "This will be lovely for dinner tonight," she said, trying to change the subject.

"Come on, Miss Pricket. Spill the beans! I insist," I said, laughing and hoping to entice her.

"Well . . ." She looked to the doorway to make sure no one was in the hallway listening. "To hear Mrs. Baddeley tell it, Mrs. Web appeared at the servants' entrance like magic, in an ominous puff of black smoke, with her bags in hand and a note from your mother explaining her new position. Your mother had arranged it all without a word to Jackson. Not even a note ahead of time to warn him of her arrival. Jackson was horrified they hadn't arranged a room before her arrival."

"Jackson may have many talents, but as far as I know fortune-telling isn't one of them," I said, making Miss Pricket laugh.

"Well, he was stoic as ever. You know Jackson." It was fun talking with Miss Pricket like this. I felt older, more mature, and she was talking to me like an adult rather than scolding me for this or that like

a child. It was fun laughing with her. I hadn't realized she was such a funny woman.

"You seem to have been spending more time
downstairs," I said.

"When your mother suggested I become your
companion I thought it would be best to get to
know them." And I thought that was a capital idea.

"Good," I said. "Gain their trust. I want to know
everything that goes on down there."

"You're sounding more like your mother with
every moment." She looked at my reflection in the
vanity mirror, a line forming between her brows for
just a moment. Then the look passed.

"Thank you, Miss Pricket," I said. "Now tell
me more."

"Well, Mrs. Baddeley was in a right state when
Mrs. Web arrived. Crying her eyes out because a
strange woman would be supervising her larders
and going through her receipts. Just this afternoon
I walked in on them in the kitchen. I heard Mrs.
Baddeley screaming at the woman, 'You keep out of
my third shelf down!'"

That made me laugh. "What's in her 'third shelf down'? Surely she wasn't referring to what I'm imagining," I said, making Miss Pricket laugh again.

"You're cheeky as ever, Miss Cruella. I think that's where she keeps her receipts," she said, laughing.

"Well, we can't have Mrs. Baddeley in tears, can we?" I said as Anita came into the room.

"I hope I'm not interrupting," she said in her customary shy way.

"Come in, Anita!" I said. "You won't believe the gossip. Miss Pricket here was telling me the Spider already has Cook in tears."

Anita blinked a couple of times. "Cook? Since when do you call Mrs. Baddeley 'Cook'?"

I didn't know. I think that might have been the first time.

"Well, she is our cook, isn't she? And that's what Mama calls her."

Anita clearly disapproved. "Well, I've never heard you call her that. I bet Arabella Slaptton calls her cook by her title rather than her name."

I thought maybe Anita was right. She usually was. But I was so eager to make Mama happy with me again. She always wanted me to be more grown-up, like a lady. Maybe this was how I could please her. Maybe if I acted like her she would like spending time with me. Maybe she would stay this time.

"Well, perhaps Arabella is on to something," I said in an offhand way, eager to change the subject.

"Who in blazes is the Spider, anyway?" Anita asked. Poor Anita. She was very smart, but sometimes she really did have trouble keeping up.

I laughed. "Oh, what's her name, Mrs. Web. The head housekeeper. The stodgy, skulking creature we met in the hall. Looks like a spider. You remember."

Anita laughed. "Yes, I suppose she does look like a spider," she said. "Shame on her for making Mrs. Baddeley cry."

"Yes," I said, laughing even harder. "I suppose Mrs. Baddeley won't be making her jellies anytime soon!" Anita and I burst into giggles all over again. Miss Pricket put a hand to her mouth.

"Come on, girls. Let's stop talking about poor Mrs. Baddeley. And stop calling Mrs. Web the Spider. It isn't very nice." I took a deep breath. It was time to take another step forward in my new relationship with Miss Pricket.

"Miss Pricket, I think I will call Mrs. Web whatever I please." Miss Pricket looked surprised, but she wisely kept her mouth shut. Then I remembered something. "Oh! Anita, I almost forgot! I have the most splendid idea for an adventure during our holiday. If Mama agrees, I think we should take a trip together. Miss Pricket can chaperone, can't you, Miss Pricket? And really, it would just be for show. You don't have to accompany Anita and me on all our excursions."

"Yes, Miss Cruella. I'd be happy to," she said, looking a little sad.

"Miss Pricket, we are going through an adjustment, aren't we? It will take a little time, don't worry. Eventually we will both find our proper places, and you will think of me as your superior rather than your charge. Though I don't think we need to be too stuffy about it, do you? Since we are almost friends, you and I." Her face fell even more. I realized then that Miss Pricket *had* thought of me as a friend. Or perhaps something more.

"Oh, Cruella," said Anita, but she stopped at that. I didn't need Anita to tell me I had hurt Miss Pricket's feelings. Well, it had to be done. I couldn't have a lady's maid who treated me like a child.

"Come on," I said, changing the subject. "Let's finish getting ready. Jackson is going to ring the gong for dinner any moment now." But they didn't move. "What?" I said. "Why are you looking at me like I killed a puppy?"

## CHAPTER VI

# THE END OF AN ERA

Christmastime was always my favorite time of year. It did something to me. It made me softer. More kindhearted. Not an affliction I fall prey to lately. But back then I loved the days leading up to Christmas almost as much as I loved the day itself.

Mama and Papa always made sure the servants made a big fuss over the winter holiday. I always looked forward to the day the tree and holiday hampers would arrive, and so did our servants. The banisters and mantels were covered with garland and every vase was filled with holiday flowers. To the left of the grand staircase, in the nook near the door leading to the morning room, was our enormous Christmas tree. It reached all the way up to the next landing. The servants always decorated it beautifully. It would be covered in delicate ornaments my family had been collecting for generations, along with tiny flickering candles, their light dancing and reflecting off the shining baubles.

Miss Pricket had invited Anita and me to help with the decorating that year. In the past I would have been eager to place the star at the top of the tree, but now I planned to take my mama's place until she was scheduled to arrive later that evening. I was determined to do all the things Mama would have done if she were there. I wanted her to come home and see I had arranged for everything perfectly. I wanted to please her. And I wanted her to see we didn't need her damnable Mrs. Web. Besides, Mama never helped the servants with decorating. She would sit in the morning room until the decorating was complete, then come out to say how lovely it was once the servants were finished. So that is what I was doing. I was wearing a lovely red dress and my jade earrings. I certainly looked the part of lady of the house.

So I let Anita do the honors, and she seemed to be having a grand time of it. I could hear her happy voice while I was in the morning room, and I almost wished I was out there with them when the hampers arrived. There was always so much excitement over the Christmas hampers before they were sent downstairs to the dungeon so Mrs. Baddeley could do her magic. Later I would hear braces of pheasants, a goose, and numerous other delights were delivered for our holiday meals. Even the servants would take a break from their usual fare of meat pies and stews to have a holiday feast of their own.

My mother had sent along gifts for our servants and a note asking that I wrap them. She would be home in time to present them all with their Christmas gifts, as was our yearly tradition. She had gotten some yards of cloth for the maids so they could make themselves new dresses, new spats for the footmen and driver, a fine broach for Miss Pricket, a new pocket watch for Jackson, and a pendant watch for

Mrs. Web. She had also sent little candied fruits and an assortment of chocolates, and had told Jackson to open some of the bottles from the cellars for their Christmas Day dinner. My mother was always generous with the servants during Christmas, and she always remarked that I should do the same when I had a household of my own one day. "A servant will forgive almost anything if you are generous during the holidays," she would say.

I let Anita amuse herself with helping the servants with the decorations while I prepared the gifts. And I took the opportunity to wrap Anita's gifts while she was busy with Miss Pricket, fussing over the tree. The house was abuzz with the sounds of laughter, music, and merrymaking, and I was becoming more excited than ever to see my mama.

"Cruella, it's time to dress for dinner." It was Miss Pricket, poking her head into the morning room, where I had been all day wrapping gifts. I'd had no idea it had gotten so late.

"Time to dress for dinner? Has Mama arrived?" I felt my heart flutter with excitement. "Ow—blast it!" I fiddled with my earring, because it was pinching something awful.

"Here, let me help you with that," Miss Pricket said, gently loosening the clasp. I immediately felt relief.

"Thank you, Miss Pricket. It's been bothering me all day." Miss Pricket gave me a sad, familiar look. I had seen that look so many times. It always meant the same thing.

"She isn't coming, is she?"

"I'm so sorry, but your mother won't be here for dinner. Cruella, dear, now that you're older I feel as if I can speak to you like a sister or friend might. It breaks my heart to see her treat you so deplorably."

I reeled in shock.

"What's that, Miss Pricket? What did you say?" I thought I hadn't heard her correctly. Surely she hadn't just spoken out against my mama.

"I'm sorry, Miss Cruella, but I know you're heartbroken. I can see it on your face. I've watched her break your heart almost every day since you were a little girl, and she's breaking it still."

"You know nothing of my heart, Miss Pricket. My mama loves me. How dare you insinuate otherwise." Looking back, I don't understand why I tried to defend my mama to her. I knew how my mama felt about me; I didn't need to convince an in-between that my mother loved me.

"She hasn't written or seen you since right after your father died. Not since she sent you away to school. That is no way to treat a daughter."

"She sends me gifts," I said, still in shock to hear Miss Pricket speaking with such candid impertinence.

"She's always given you gifts, Miss Cruella. That is all she has ever given you. It's all she will ever give you, the heartless, cruel, and horrible woman she is. Beautiful gifts, and nothing of herself."

This time she had crossed the line. She presumed too much. She let her in-between status lead her to believe we were true friends—*sisters*, even. She'd let it lead her to believe she could speak that way to me about my mother. I didn't have to say another word. She saw the look on my face, and we both knew there was no mending this. I could never look at her the same way again. I could never trust her. She had to go.

The in-between tried to mutter more apologies, but I cut her off before she could say another word. I hastily stuffed some banknotes I got from the desk in an envelope and put it in her hand.

"Here is your severance, Miss Pricket."

"You're dismissing me?" Her mouth hung open. Though I couldn't fathom her thinking I would keep her on after everything she had said.

"Of course I am. Don't be foolish. I couldn't possibly keep you on."

It was such a strange yet liberating feeling taking charge in this way. I realized in that moment I was on the precipice of a new chapter in my life. I was becoming a lady, and with that came enormous responsibility. I felt very sure my mama would be proud of me for taking charge in this way. Not only for taking control over my own life but for defending her. Miss Pricket had, until that moment, been a very important part of my life, but I couldn't have her or anyone else creating a wedge between me and my mama. She had overstepped the mark, that invisible line that divides us from our servants. And it was a very important lesson—I would not let myself become emotionally involved with anyone from my staff again.

"But I have nowhere to go." Her eyes filled with tears, but my heart had closed off to her. Her tears didn't sway me.

"That is of no consequence to me. You may stay the night in your quarters. But I don't wish to see you here tomorrow morning."

She said nothing. She just stood there in disbelief, tears rolling down her face. She looked utterly heartbroken. "Off you go then. Goodbye, Miss Pricket." As she turned her back to leave, I could see she was sobbing even harder, but silently. She turned the knob slowly, shaking as she opened the door. "Enjoy your new life, Miss Pricket. Oh, and when you leave tomorrow, be sure to leave by the servants' entrance." She looked back at me, tears streaming down her face.

## The End of an Era

"I loved you so well, Cruella. And I hope with all my heart you don't become a cruel, sad, and lonely woman, *like your mother*."

I slammed the door behind her, closing that chapter of my life once and for all.

## CHAPTER VII

# CHRISTMAS EVE

In my household the servants had their holiday celebration on Christmas Eve. It had been that way since I was a girl, and I didn't see any reason to change it. When my grandparents were alive my parents and I would dine with them at their estate, leaving the house to the servants so they could have a celebration of their own without having to fuss over us. Later, after my grandparents passed, we would dine with friends of my father or mother. This year, with my mama away and Papa gone, and with no invitations to speak of, Anita and I found ourselves home on Christmas Eve.

We couldn't very well go out for dinner without

a proper escort now that Miss Pricket had been dismissed. So we were forced to stay home. I spoke to Jackson about it, assuring him Anita and I would be fine if Mrs. Baddeley prepared us something and sent it up on a tray. I didn't want to ruin their celebration. And I especially wanted to extend some holiday cheer since they were all likely curious what happened with Miss Pricket. The last thing I needed was Mama coming home to an empty house with no servants. I counted on Jackson to spread the word about Miss Pricket and dispel any fears they may have about the De Vil household cutting back on servants like many of the larger households had been doing as of late.

"She spoke unkindly to me about Lady De Vil," was all I had to say. Jackson understood. And I could tell he thought I had done the right thing.

As I was talking to Jackson, the Spider came skittering into the room like a walking nightmare on two legs. "Miss Cruella, I have advised downstairs that you and Miss Anita will be home this evening. Please ring if you need anything at all. Dinner will be served in the dining room at eight." I blinked at her, trying to decide if she was as frightful as my mind had originally conjured.

She was. Frightful and odious.

"As I was just telling Jackson, something on a tray for dinner will be fine, Mrs. Web. I don't want to interrupt your festivities this evening. Anita and I will be quite happy to spend a quiet evening together. We will have our Christmas dinner tomorrow as we always have."

"But Lady De Vil gave other instructions, Miss Cruella, and Mrs. Baddeley has been downstairs cooking all day. She's created a feast. I wouldn't want to disappoint her."

"So this is something you and Lady De Vil discussed, but you didn't see fit to share it with me until now?" I had broken protocol. I had admitted I didn't know something. I'd admitted my mother didn't share her plans with me. But I continued without missing a beat.

"But what about your celebration? I had intended to present you with your gifts this evening before your Christmas meal. If you're all busy preparing a feast and cleaning up afterwards, when will you have time for your celebration?"

"During breakfast tomorrow, as your mother instructed."

"During breakfast? Oh, that won't do, Mrs. Web. Does that sound fair to you, Anita?" Anita shook her head, but she didn't say anything. Sweet Anita hated conflict. "I'd hate to break with tradition, Mrs. Web," I continued. "And I don't want to deprive the staff of their festivities. They work so hard all year, and this is their treat for being so devoted and loyal."

I waited for Mrs. Web to challenge me, but she just pursed her lips and stayed silent.

"Then it's decided. We will proceed as usual, as we have for many years before you joined our household." I wanted things to be as they were in the years before Papa passed and before Mama went away. Everything had gone so terribly wrong after Papa's death, and I thought that maybe if I could recapture our Christmas celebrations of the past, and not let this vile woman change everything, Mama would come around to me. Of course, I couldn't have been more wrong. I was flying in the face of my mother's instructions. But the young don't always make the wisest decisions, no matter how well intended they may be.

The Spider just looked at me, unblinking. I assumed she didn't want to contradict me *or* my mother. So she stood silently until Jackson broke the uncomfortable silence.

"Miss Cruella, I know Mrs. Baddeley would be terribly upset if her holiday feast went to waste. She's been hard at work all day."

"I have an idea!" Anita said. Sweet Anita. Caring Anita. Always looking out for the underdog. Always wanting to do good. She would do anything to make people happy, especially people she was fond of. Funny how, in the end, she couldn't do the same for me.

But I'm jumping ahead. That part of the story doesn't come until later.

"I saw how much food Mrs. Baddeley was

preparing downstairs," Anita said. "It's far too much for just the two of us. There's more than enough for everyone. What if we invite the staff to join us for Christmas dinner? And afterwards they can continue the celebration downstairs as they like."

"That's very kind of you, Miss Anita, but rather unorthodox," said the odious Spider. "Lady De Vil would be angry to learn the servants dined upstairs."

The last thing I wanted to do was agree with that woman, even though she was right. My mother would be livid. But the look on Anita's face was so sincere, and I wanted to make her happy. I wanted to do something nice for her after everything she'd done for me since my father had passed away. So I suggested an alternative.

"Well, if the staff wouldn't object, perhaps Anita and I could join you downstairs and we can share the meal together." I looked to Jackson because I valued his opinion more. Unlike Mrs. Web, he had been with our family for many years, even before I was born. The only other person who had known me that long was Miss Pricket. Perhaps if things hadn't gone the way they did, I would be asking her about Christmas dinner now.

"We wouldn't stay downstairs with you all evening, mind you. Just for dinner, and then we would leave you to continue your celebration after we've gone upstairs. We wouldn't need you for the rest of the evening, I promise, as long as Jackson sets out the grog tray, and perhaps a little tray of sandwiches in the event we get peckish before bed," I said, looking at Jackson and hoping he would agree.

I thought that was the most suitable way out of our dilemma. "And before dinner I can give you our gifts. I am sure Lady De Vil wishes she could be here to present them to you herself, but I will have to do."

"Miss Cruella." The Spider's face was pinched tight. "This is very out of the ordinary, and I'm not sure your mother would approve." I smiled my sweetest smile at the woman. Looking back on all of this now, I have to wonder if I wasn't just happy to be in opposition to Mrs. Web. I wasn't even thinking about how all of this would make Mama feel. I had convinced myself she would be happy I took charge and made sure to uphold our family traditions. But I'm not sure that was my strongest motivation.

"I'd like to hear what Jackson thinks. He's been taking care of this family since before I was born, and I think he is the best judge. Jackson, do you agree with Mrs. Web? Do you think my mother would object if we combined Christmas celebrations this evening?"

Jackson narrowed his eyes at the Spider. "I do believe she would, Miss Cruella."

"But Jackson, I was so looking forward to presenting you with your gifts, and I don't want to deprive the staff of their celebration. I will be terribly disappointed if we can't find a way around this."

Jackson smiled. He could never deny me anything. Not since I was a child, and I really wanted to win this battle with Mrs. Web.

"Well, Miss Cruella, the last thing I want to do is disappoint you."

I had always liked Jackson. Out of all our staff

he was most like a member of the family. Always there. Always loyal. Always on my side. And after my father passed, always looking out for me. It's true, I had resented his attentions and the somber looks he gave when my mama set off on her trip, but he never spoke ill of her. In that moment, as his usually somber face broke into an indulgent smile just for me, he reminded me so much of my papa, who I was missing terribly. I didn't understand why it had taken me so long to see Jackson in this way. *Really* see him. The way I had seen him when I was young. I'd adored him when I was small. He always took a special interest in me. And he was doing so again.

Perhaps it was the magic of Christmas, or perhaps I was just happy to have someone to side with me against the Spider, but I saw Jackson clearly that day. And we had won the battle together, Jackson and I. We were allies in combat against the wretched Spider.

"Then it's all set! We will all have Christmas dinner together downstairs. It will be a scream!"

$\mathcal{B}$efore dinner, Anita and I changed. I remember feeling liberated by not having to dress up for dinner. If we had been eating upstairs in the dining room with Mama we would have had to dress like we were having the Queen for dinner. As it was, we both wore something simple and comfortable. I didn't even wear the earrings Papa gave me.

The servants' hall was decorated with a colorful garland made of paper rings that were chain-linked together, alternating red and green. There were festive bits of holly and sprigs of pine tied with red ribbons that hung in the doorways. In the corner near the fireplace was a small tree, decorated with strings of popcorn and cranberries, and faded gold beads that glistened in the firelight.

It was much more cheerful downstairs than I remembered. I hadn't spent much time in the servants' hall; most of my visits were to the kitchen. Anita and I said hello to Mrs. Baddeley as we came down the stairs, but we were shooed away and told to close our eyes. "I'm making something special for you, dears! No peeking!"

Anita and I laughed. It felt like the old days.

The kitchen was separated from the servants' hall by a large hutch that was built into the wall. There was a hinged, shuttered window in the middle of the hutch that could be opened so those inside the servants' hall and the kitchen could pass things back and forth and speak to each other without having to go around to the other entrance.

The hall had a long dining table that was already set with old-fashioned Churchill Blue Willow patterned dishes. On the other side of the room was a large fireplace and mantel, with two chairs facing the fire, which I assumed were Jackson's and Mrs. Baddeley's. Between the chairs was a small wooden round table, and there were a number of small pillows on an old rug I remembered having in the morning room when I was a child. I supposed that is where the other servants sat when they weren't at the dining table, perhaps to warm themselves by the fire while drinking their cocoa before bedtime. It was a cozy place.

"I'm so happy you decided to have Christmas dinner down here with the staff, Cruella," said Anita, beaming. "It would have been lonely upstairs just the two of us. I always felt Christmas was a time to spend with your family." Anita saw me flinch at the word *family*, but I wasn't angry with her. I understood what she meant. It *was* a time for family, and I was missing my papa and mama more than ever.

"I understand. You think of Mrs. Baddeley and Jackson as family."

"I thought of Miss Pricket as family as well." Her voice was sad, but there was something else in there, too.

"I know you're disappointed, Anita, but I don't wish to talk about Miss Pricket. Not now, anyway. Not in front of the other servants."

"But you *do* think of them as family, don't you?" she asked.

I thought about it. "Perhaps not in the same way you do, Anita. But I love that they treat you like a member of the family. Because to me you are a dear sister."

"And you are mine, Cruella. I don't know where I'd be without you."

Oh, how it breaks my heart to think Anita and I are no longer close. That she no longer loves me as she once did. But I shouldn't digress. Those were happy days. At least I thought they were. The days before Anita betrayed me, when she was practically my world.

But back to Christmas Eve. Anita and I were in the servants' hall taking a look around when Mrs. Baddeley abruptly opened the shutters, her red, happy face peering through the hutch window.

"Miss Cruella, hello, my dear. I'm sorry I shooed you away."

I smiled at the woman. "I understand you're up to your old tricks again, whipping up some sort of surprise! I bet I can guess what it might be!" I imagined raspberry jellies as far as the eye could see, and laughed to myself.

"Never you mind about that, Cruella! You will just have to wait!" She closed the shutter doors again with a dramatic and playful snap. Anita smiled at me.

"See, she isn't so bad. I know she annoys you, but she's actually a very sweet woman, and she loves you very much."

It had never occurred to me that Mrs. Baddeley loved me. Not until Anita said so. And it made me wonder—had I had it all wrong? Maybe she had always loved me, the way Jackson had, since I was a little girl. Why had it taken me so long to understand that? I suddenly felt so ashamed for sending Miss Pricket away. It was almost like the woman I had been in that moment was an entirely different person than the woman I was now. And she had come out without my knowledge or permission. I didn't like that person inside me who said and did mean, awful things. But sometimes it felt as if I had no control over her.

I desperately wanted to talk to Anita about it, but not then. It would have to wait until after dinner. The thoughts swirling through my head were too strange to say out loud in this cheerful room. Something within me was changing, something I couldn't explain.

But there wasn't time to slip away and talk. Everyone was making their way to the servants' hall and taking their places around the table.

I was offered Jackson's seat at the head of the table, but I declined, choosing to sit by Anita with our backs to the hutch so we would be facing the fireplace and the little tree. "No, Jackson, that place of honor is for you. I won't take it. I'm your guest this evening," I said. Mrs. Baddeley seemed touched by my saying that, and I wondered if there wasn't something between them. I'd often heard stories of butlers and cooks finding love in their older age. Sometimes it was the butler and the head house-keeper. But something about the way Mrs. Baddeley looked at Jackson made me wonder if there was some spark there, and I wondered if it was mutual. Jackson, of course, was too stoic to let on even if he did have feelings for the woman.

As I looked around the table, I noticed someone was missing. "Where is Mrs. Web?" I asked.

"Oh, she takes her meals in her sitting room," said Mrs. Baddeley, rolling her eyes and making a funny gesture with her hands as if she were the fanciest woman alive.

"Oh, does she? So Miss High-and-Mighty is too grand to eat with the other servants?" I asked, making everyone laugh and breaking the ice. It was so lovely to see all of them at the table, smiling and enjoying themselves. All of the housemaids were talking and giggling when Mrs. Baddeley interrupted their reverie.

"Mr. Jackson, could we perhaps have Jean turn on the wireless? I think there is a Christmas concert tonight."

Jackson's face brightened.

"That's a wonderful idea, Mrs. Baddeley, and while we're at it, I don't see the harm in getting a bottle from the cellar. It is Christmas, after all," he said with a wink.

It was such a grand evening of eating, drinking, and listening to Christmas music on the wireless. Anita had thought to bring down some Christmas crackers, so everyone was wearing festive paper hats while we dined on Mrs. Baddeley's magnificent feast.

"I would like to propose a toast," I said, standing up. "To Mrs. Baddeley, for this delicious meal!"

"To Mrs. Baddeley!" everyone cheered. Even Jackson looked festive, wearing his paper crown merrily, even though we'd had to talk him into wearing it at first. It was a happy night, full of laughter, food, and, yes, family.

I loved seeing all their happy faces, all of them gathered together. Eating downstairs was so much more fun than eating up in the dining room. No one was scolding me to act like a lady. Everyone passed great bowls and platters of food around the table, helping themselves to as much as they liked. Jackson carved the beef Wellington, like he was the father of this little family. Mrs. Baddeley had made sure to make all of mine and Anita's favorites.

"Oh, Mrs. Baddeley, you wonderful dear woman, you remembered how much I love your cheese straws!" Anita cried with delight. Mrs. Baddeley smiled between bites of beef Wellington.

"Oh yes, my dear. I have remembered all your favorites. And Miss Cruella's as well."

"I see that, Mrs. Baddeley," I said, looking at the side table laden with lemon tarts, little cookies covered in powdered sugar, a rum and walnut cake, and a three-tiered cake covered in white icing. "And the pudding looks amazing. But I wonder if we will have room after eating all of this?" I scooped more roasted potatoes and carrots onto my plate.

"Oh, you haven't seen the half of it. You haven't even seen my surprise," she said.

"There's more?" Anita asked. "I can't even imagine how that's possible!"

Then I remembered. Their gifts! "I was so excited for our little party I forgot to present you with your gifts! Let me run upstairs and get them!"

"No, Miss Cruella." Jackson put a gentle hand on my shoulder. "Sit. We still have pudding. Mrs. Baddeley has been working on your surprise all day. Besides, you are our gift this evening. We're so happy to have you and Miss Anita with us."

"Yes!" said Jean.

"Oh, please stay. You can give us our gifts later," said Paulie.

151

"See, these people love you, Cruella," Anita said under her breath. "Who else could get Jackson to wear a paper crown?"

"Well, Mrs. Baddeley, I think it's time Paulie brings in your crowning Christmas achievement," said Jackson, giving Mrs. Baddeley a little nudge and wink.

"Yes, Paulie. Go on. It's on the silver tray sitting on the counter," she said, adding, "Jean, go help her. And don't go stumbling and ruining Miss Cruella's surprise." I laughed. Mrs. Baddeley wasn't a terrible woman at all. If Jackson was the father of this family, surely Mrs. Baddeley was its mother.

"I'm sure they will do just fine, Mrs. Baddeley," said Jackson.

And then it arrived. The largest, most magnificent jelly I had ever seen. It was raspberry, of course, and suspended within were cherries and tiny oranges. It didn't seem possible to create such a large jelly without breaking it as it came out of the mold. She had decorated it beautifully, with thick whipped cream flowers. I felt like a little girl again.

It was the most wonderful surprise of all. A strange feeling pricked at my eyes, and I realized they were wet with tears. And in that moment, I decided I liked jellies more than almost anything, because this dear woman had made them for me.

"Oh, Mrs. Baddeley. I love it. Thank you," I said getting up and kissing her on the cheek. "I am so thankful to have you, and for spending this evening with all of you." Mrs. Baddeley embraced me tightly. When I came away, I had flour on my dress. But this time, I didn't care.

After dinner the servants talked Anita and me into staying for a glass of mulled wine, and to sing Christmas songs before we went upstairs. My heart felt full and my face was flushed. My ghosts weren't ghosts. They were people, and they loved me. Anita was right. They were my family.

And then the bell rang.

We weren't expecting guests. But Jackson quickly put on his jacket so he could go upstairs to see who it was. "It's likely just children caroling, Miss Cruella. I won't be more than a moment."

"Oh, wouldn't it be lovely if we all went up to give them a little something? The poor mites," I said.

"Oh, yes!" said Paulie. "I know. Let's give them some of the chocolates your mother sent us. It would be a nice treat for them."

Mrs. Baddeley chimed in. "Jean, go get a basket from the kitchen. One of my wicker shopping baskets, and bring it here, along with a length of some wax paper. We can wrap up some of those cookies for them as well."

"Oh, this is so exciting," I said to Anita. I felt like we were on an adventure as we headed upstairs with our basket of chocolates and cookies to give to the singing children. We all stood there assembled, ready to surprise them. "Okay, Jackson, open the door," I said, feeling like I might burst from the pure joy of the evening. It was the happiest I had felt since Papa died.

Jackson opened the door, but it wasn't children who were waiting.

It was Mama.

"Jackson! What is the meaning of this?" My mother was livid as she took in the sight of us with our lopsided paper hats, flushed faces, and joyous expressions. Then her eyes landed on me. I had never seen her so angry.

"Mama! We weren't expecting you!" I said. Part of me was so happy to see her after all this time. Part of me, too, felt a sense of foreboding form in the pit of my stomach.

"Clearly! Look at yourselves! My goodness, Cruella, you're a mess! What in heavens is going on? Explain yourself!"

"When we heard the bell upstairs we thought it was caroling children at the door," I said, my shoulders falling at her anger and disapproval. "We thought it would be festive to bring them some sweets."

"I don't understand, Cruella! What were you doing downstairs?" She took in the flour all over my dress. The flour I hadn't even cared about just minutes before. My mama was so angry at me; I couldn't bring myself to tell her we had been down with the servants celebrating Christmas. "Cruella, answer me! Whose idea was this?"

Anita was the one who spoke up. "It was my idea, Lady De Vil," she said in her soft, sweet voice. Anita was always braver than I gave her credit for.

You have to watch out for the quiet ones. Take some advice from me. The quiet, observant girls are the deadliest.

My mother just looked at Anita as if she didn't know her, as if she hadn't spoken, and directed her words at Jackson. "Jackson, send the staff downstairs." I wanted to say I hadn't had the chance to give the staff their gifts yet. I wanted to say that it was my idea. But I couldn't make the words come out. It turned out I wasn't as brave as Anita. "Cruella, I'd like to speak with you in the morning room. Anita, if you would please excuse us?" Anita looked over her shoulder at me as she went up the stairs. I could tell she felt bad, and she was worried for me. I flashed her a reassuring smile as I made my way into the morning room with my mama. But we both knew my smile was fake.

Mama was seething. "Clearly this girl is a horrible influence on you. Six months away, and I come home to see you looking like this? Look at the state of you. What are you wearing, Cruella? Why are you dressed like a common house girl? You aren't even wearing the earrings your father gave you!"

It was true. I hadn't dressed up. I was wearing one of my plainer dresses, something I would usually wear on outings in the park or woods. "Walking clothes," my mother called them. I hadn't wanted to dress up and be flashy. I'd wanted to fit in downstairs. And now I felt as if I didn't belong in the morning room with my mama. My face felt warm, and I wondered if it was red.

"This is too much, Cruella. Too much. I sent you to that school to become a lady, not a common housemaid. Clearly Anita has been a bad influence on you! I should never have arranged for her to join you," she said, pouring herself a glass of sherry and sitting on the leather couch in her usual spot.

"That's not true, Mother!"

"Not true? Since when do you dress like this on

Christmas Eve? I gave Mrs. Web explicit instructions on how this evening should go, and you defied my wishes. I don't even know who you are." Mrs. Web. Of course. She had tipped my mother off.

"She told you?"

"Of course she told me. She's my head housekeeper. She is my eyes and ears when I am away. You are not to act the lady of the house with her, do you understand? She enforces my will when I'm not here to do it myself."

"She's a horrible woman, Mother. She wanted the servants to give up their holiday party. I couldn't believe those were your wishes. What's the harm in having a little party for the servants? You and Papa told me about the servants' balls Grandmama used to have in the old days. What's the difference between that and what we did tonight?"

"All the difference in the world! That was a grand estate, Cruella, a world of its own. With old traditions that went back too many generations to count. We live in the city. Dining in the kitchen with servants just isn't done. What if the other ladies hear about this? What if Anita tells her guardian's daughters? This kind of news travels through society. We'd be a laughingstock."

She didn't give me a moment to reply or try to defend myself. "I have made a decision, Cruella. I don't want you going back to that school. I think it's time for you to come out into society. We need to find you a husband at once! Someone who will take you in hand and curb this attitude of yours."

I couldn't believe she was saying this. "What attitude?" I asked.

"You don't think I hear what you have been up to at school? Your threats to the headmistress and your constant snotty attitude, haughtiness with the other students in your avid devotion and defense of Anita? Alienating you from all the proper young women I sent you there to meet. This has to stop! I don't want you seeing that girl anymore, do you understand?"

And for the first time ever, I stood up to my mother.

"Anita is my best friend!"

"She is not your friend! She is little better than a servant. And I will not have her influencing you in this way!"

"The party was my idea, Mother, not Anita's."

But my mother didn't believe me.

"Don't lie to me, Cruella! And don't argue with me. I am taking you out of school, and you won't be seeing that Anita any longer."

"You can't keep me from seeing Anita, Mother, you can't! And please let me finish school. I was so looking forward to going back."

"It's not possible, Cruella, not after your embarrassing yourself and our family by defending that common girl! And now I come home to find her here. And from what I hear from Mrs. Web, she was practically living here all summer before you left for school?"

"Miss Pricket said you didn't mind. You were away! I had no one!"

"Miss Pricket didn't tell me. That woman was always overindulgent with you. Giving you whatever you wanted behind my back. Insisting I see you in the afternoons before I went out. Insisting she take you gifts for your birthday, sneaking that Anita into the house when I wasn't here. I was planning to dismiss her myself, but it seems you beat me to it."

"Well, I regret that now," I said. And I did. I saw now how it was Miss Pricket who had looked out for me. Who was responsible for all my happy moments growing up. And suddenly, all of Miss Pricket's sad looks made sense.

"I want Anita to leave first thing in the morning, Cruella. I won't have her in my house another night. Having her here gives me the most disturbing feeling. Like something predatory is circling my house."

"Mother, please! What can I do to make this up to you? What can I do to make you let Anita stay?" But there wasn't anything I could say or do. She had set her mind and heart against Anita, and it was breaking mine.

"Cruella, it's bad enough Anita has practically been living here, but for you to actually *dine* downstairs with the servants. For goodness' sake, we don't have those sorts of—"

"People, Mother. Those sorts of people," I said. I realized then that I had been just as guilty as my mother had. All my life, I'd thought of them as ghosts or in-betweens, when really, they were people just like me. They were my family. Maybe even more so than the one I was born into. And here she was forbidding me from seeing my only friend, and trying to make me distance myself from the only people who had really ever cared for me, besides Papa.

"They're not people, Cruella. Not like you and me! And I won't have you socializing with them. It was one thing when you were a little girl, but you're a lady now! And I won't have Anita influencing you any longer! You're seventeen, and will be almost eighteen after the season. Old enough to marry. The sooner we get you a household of your own and a husband to rule you, all the better. And that's the end of it!"

## CHAPTER VIII

# DISTINGUISH YOURSELF

I didn't return to school after the break, and Mother had made it impossible for me to see Anita. She was away at school while I was back in London, attending every ball and social event my mother could throw at me. It was a nightmare.

I was paraded around like a peacock, decked out in feathers and glittering jewels, and made to endure an endless parade of tedious young men. Looking back, I feel I should have found a way to enjoy myself more. But I resented my mother for keeping me away from Anita. I was broken-hearted, and I made my mother pay for it at every opportunity.

Before she had come home on Christmas Eve I had been longing to mend my relationship with her. Now, here she was devoting all her time to me, buying me the most beautiful clothes and finally giving me the attention I craved, but it felt so wrong. I fought her on it every step of the way.

I corresponded with Anita several times a week, each of us keeping each other up to date on our daily lives and counting the days until she would be home again. Anita's letters back were always so cheerful. She was, of course, doing well in school, and she was pleasantly surprised that she liked the new girl who had taken my place in her room. I hated the idea of Anita spending time with her new roommate, taking our walks, having our conversations, and reading our book of fairy tales. I wanted her back home where she belonged.

After I was presented at court, the endless balls and glittering social events began.

My mother was just itching for me to accept one of the various proposals I had received from my many suitors. I was a catch, as they say. Titled, and soon to be in possession of an obscene amount of money. Over the course of the season my mother invited a legion of young gentlemen over for dinner, sometimes inviting them to stay for the weekend if they were visiting London from somewhere out of town. Socialite mercenary mothers went to great lengths to find their daughters suitable husbands, and she was relentless.

Every morning it was the same. She'd come into the dining room and tell me what our schedule was for the day—that is, if we didn't have a visitor we were entertaining. "Good morning, Cruella!" her voice would ring out, and I knew I was in for a matchmaking onslaught.

"Good morning, Mother." She would grab her coffee and sit down with it at the table with her diary.

"I miss the days when you called me your mama."

I would roll my eyes and say something like, "Well, as you say, I am a lady now. I'm simply speaking like one." She would pretend she didn't hear me and list off our daily events from her diary.

One particular morning, we happened to have a visitor staying with us. He hadn't made his way to the dining room yet.

"Jackson, is Lord Silverton awake?" Mother asked as Jackson and Jean placed a selection of pastries, fresh fruit, and eggs on the serving table.

"Yes, Lady De Vil, he will be down shortly." Jackson put the newspaper at the place reserved for him. "I thought Lord Silverton would like to read the paper."

I smiled at Jackson. "Yes, perhaps he can take a look at the train schedule. I'm sure he's eager to get back home."

My mother set her cup of coffee down with an annoyed thump. "Cruella. He's a very fine young man."

"Yes, Mother, I am sure he is. But he is also incredibly boring."

"Cruella, it is the lady's job to keep the conversation moving. If you're bored then you're not doing your job correctly." She took a pile of invitations from a silver tray Jackson presented to her.

"Oh, I ask him questions, and he's all too happy to talk about himself. I just don't want to listen to another of his tedious stories, Mother. I can only listen to so many tales of horses, fox hunting, and shooting quail. We have nothing in common," I said, sipping my coffee and deciding if I wanted to eat anything. I felt queasy at the thought of enduring another conversation with Lord Silverton. Oh, he was handsome enough, I suppose. All golden and fair, with delicate features, blue eyes and all that. Perfect and boring, like vanilla ice cream.

"Your father and I had nothing in common, and look at us," she said, giving me the side-eye over her coffee cup.

"Well, I'd be happy to find a man like Papa if I had a mind to marry," I said. "But as far as Lord Boredington goes, there isn't enough money in all the world that would make me want to marry him." I couldn't help laughing at my own joke. *Someone* had to laugh, because my mother didn't seem to find it amusing in the least.

"Of course you're going to marry, Cruella. And do stop making up insulting names for people."

"Yes, Mother." But she couldn't sway me.

I had set myself against the idea of marriage long before. It had become quite clear to me that I hated being told what to do. I wanted to be independent. "No man worth his salt will be willing to let his children take his wife's name, Mother," I said.

"Well, my dear Cruella, if you find a rich enough husband like Lord Silverton then you won't have to worry about that." I couldn't believe she was suggesting I go against my papa's wishes.

"I made a promise to Papa. That's the end of it, Mother. If I ever do get married, and I doubt I ever will, I will not take his name." Mother closed her diary and tapped it with her pen.

"Well, Cruella, the Queen didn't take her husband's name, and look how that's turned out. Do you want to live your life resented by your husband?"

I laughed.

"Well, Mother, that's one of the reasons I don't intend to marry." I thought on it. "And the Queen gets to be the Queen. If I got to be queen, being resented by my husband is a sacrifice I'd be willing to make."

"That's cheeky, Cruella, even for you."

Just then Lord Boringpants came into the dining room. "Well, that is disappointing news, Lady Cruella," he said, smiling at me in a way he obviously thought was dashing. "But I bet I can change your mind. I think your mother is in possession of an invitation from my own, inviting you to our estate for the weekend." He was beaming, way too chipper for someone who hadn't had their coffee yet. I imagined myself married to this relentlessly happy man and it made my stomach churn.

"Oh, I don't know, Lord Silverton," I said, but he pressed on.

"It will be the most topping weekend, Lady Cruella. I know you won't be able to say no to my proposal once you see your future home." I thought my mother was going to jump out of her seat and start dancing the jig right there on the dining room table. (Not that she would ever do such a thing, but honestly, I have never seen her that happy in my life.)

"Cruella!" she crowed. "You didn't tell me Lord Silverton proposed. Jackson, bring the champagne!" I just sat there, drinking my coffee and laughing.

"Jackson, don't bother. We won't be needing the champagne." My mother's face fell lower than one of Mrs. Baddeley's failed soufflés.

"Cruella! Must you always be such a beast? You've not even given Lord Silverton a chance." The fact was Lord Stuffypants hadn't even proposed. But he was quite transparent in his desire to. Didn't he understand women like a bit of mystery?

"Don't fret, Lady De Vil," Lord Blunderpants said, sweeping his Prince Charming hair out of his face. "I haven't proposed, not yet. I plan to after I woo her with the grandest of weekends at my parents' estate. I know she won't be able to say no."

"I couldn't possibly go, Lord Silverton. We have

far too many obligations already. I couldn't possibly put them off. It would be rude."

"Oh, I could call them all, Cruella. Just leave that to me," my mother said. "You have your weekend with Lord Silverton." I was painted into a corner. I couldn't get out of it without being rude, and I feared I could only push things so far with my mother. I had no other choice.

"Lord Silverton, I would love nothing more than to accept your invitation," I said without emotion.

"Oh, this is so topping, Lady Cruella! I'm going to call Mother and tell her you're coming."

I smiled and boldly took his hand. "I had no idea you were so progressive, Lord Silverton. I never imagined you would be the sort of man who wouldn't mind taking his wife's name." For the first time since his arrival, Lord Silverton's smile faded.

"What's that, Lady Cruella?" he asked. "I'm sure I must have heard you incorrectly." I smirked at my mother.

"No, Lord Silverton, I'm afraid you heard me correctly. You see, my papa's last wish was that I keep my family name. I am the last of the De Vil line." Lord Silverton looked thoroughly disappointed, and a little frightened. He had all but proposed, and I could see his wheels spinning, wondering if I was going to make him stick to his word. I didn't mind watching him squirm a little longer before I let him off the hook.

"Well, Mother would never allow it," he said, fidgeting. "Are you absolutely sure, Lady Cruella? Is there no way around it?"

I looked down, feigning that I was terribly disappointed.

"I'm afraid there isn't." And then I took a gamble. "Well, I do suppose there is one way around it," I said, looking up at him with sad eyes. "I could give up my inheritance. But I suppose that wouldn't matter to a great family like yours." Lord Silverton's expression turned to something else entirely. The brilliant, smiling facade was replaced by anger and frustration. I had heard his family had been struggling to keep up their estate, and they were considering selling off some of the land to keep it going. It was a miracle they had held on to that mammoth of an albatross as long as they had. I had seen so many families brought to ruin by simply trying to hold on to their family's enormous, burdensome estates. The last ditch effort was always marrying money. And I had calculated correctly.

"Ah, I just remembered, I have to catch the next train. . . ."

I patted Lord Penniless on the hand.

"No need to go on, Lord Silverton. I completely understand. I release you of any understanding we may have had." And he literally dashed out of the room with barely a thank you and a goodbye to my mother. She was livid.

"Cruella! How dare you frighten him away like that?"

I walked to the sideboard and got myself another cup of coffee while she told me off. "You heard him, Lady Silverton wouldn't have allowed him to marry a woman who kept her name," I responded.

"Would it be so tragic to go against your father's wishes?" she asked.

"Mother! His family needs him to marry some-one with money. He wasn't interested in me, he was interested in my fortune."

She slammed her hand on the table, making the coffee cups and saucers rattle.

"I would have settled on an amount with his family. You wouldn't be going into the marriage penniless, I would have arranged a yearly dress allowance for you as well. This is why you must leave these sorts of things to me, my dear. I would have made all the arrangements." It was in that moment I knew my decision to never marry was the right one. The idea of my mother arranging a mar-riage in some stuffy drawing room with some lord or baron's mother, agreeing to settle on an amount of money for them to take me off her hands like some kind of prized cow was laughable. It reminded me of Miss Upturn, and Arabella Slaptton, and everything I hated.

"Mother, I will never marry! Never! So you might as well give up the idea entirely." That wasn't the life I wanted. "Besides, Papa wanted me to be happy."

I still had it in my mind that I would spend my days with Anita as my companion. Traveling the world together, seeing everything we had ever read about in our most cherished books. And I had a notion to find that distant and magical land where my earrings had been found by that ill-fated pirate, the one my father told me about the night he gave them to me. I was going to spring it on Anita the next time we saw each other. A grand pirate adventure. Curses, and heroes, and villains, just like one of Princess Tulip's fairy tales.

It would be just the two of us. No stuffy lords or meddlesome mothers. From that point on I refused to go to any more balls or social engagements my mother tried to arrange. And I refused to wear any of my fabulous furs or feathers or any of the other things my mother had heaped upon me for the purposes of snagging a husband. I couldn't stand to touch anything she had given me. She had even forced me into gaudy diamonds that dripped from my ears; I hadn't worn my cherished jade earrings since Christmas. Poor Papa. He wouldn't approve of what Mother was trying to do. He wouldn't want me married to some boring man with a boring name who spent his idle days hunting, flitting from place to place depending on the season like a migrating bird. A man completely lacking in imagination. I'm sure he would want someone who loved my independent spirit. And someone who loved me for me, not just my money.

My mother, frustrated that I refused to see any more of her suitors, went off on one of her trips and announced she wouldn't be back for some time. I was thrilled. I could have Anita stay with me. I called her the moment my mother left for her trip to Paris or wherever it was she'd run off to. I was almost sure she wouldn't be returning home in time to celebrate my eighteenth birthday, and honestly, I was secretly hoping she wouldn't. Everything was as it should be. My solicitor, Sir Huntley, had sent over the paperwork that detailed my new allowance once I turned eighteen. I didn't need mama anymore, and I found myself feeling much more at home without her there. I was the lady of the house while she was away.

## Distinguish Yourself

❖ ❖ ❖ ❖

Before I knew it, the school term was over and Anita was to return home. Back to Belgrave Square, where she belonged. With me. And with her extended family, my servants. Anita had always been close to them, and since our holiday meal together I had felt closer to them than ever before. Mrs. Baddeley and Jackson had kept me sane throughout mother's husband-hunting season, what with Jackson's commiserating looks and my sneaking down to the kitchen to talk with Mrs. Baddeley about the awful bores my mother was throwing at me. But now I would have my Anita back. I couldn't wait. The day had finally arrived.

I stood in the entryway for what felt like an eternity waiting for Anita to arrive. I couldn't just sit in the morning room waiting for her to be ushered in and announced by Jackson. She wasn't a mere guest. She was my family. My only family, now that Papa was gone and Mama had all but given up on me. Then I finally heard the car pulling up out front. I didn't even let Jackson open the door entirely before I dashed over to give her a hug.

"Oh, Anita! I am so happy to see you!" I threw my arms around her.

She looked more radiant than ever. We wrapped our arms around each other, holding on tightly before letting go. She had the most beautiful smile on her face. She was home.

"Cruella! Happy birthday!" she said. I had almost forgotten it was my birthday. I was too excited about her visit.

"Miss Anita," Jackson said, "I will have your things taken upstairs. I'm sure Mrs. Baddeley is eager to say hello if you'd like to go down and see her. I think she might have a little surprise for you." He gave her a little wink.

"Oh, yes," said Anita. "Come on, Cruella." She took my hand.

"What are you up to?" I asked. "Why is Jackson ushering us downstairs?" Anita just laughed.

"It's just as he said. I'm sure he realizes I am excited to see Mrs. Baddeley. Come on."

I remember holding Anita's small hand in mine as we walked down the stairs. It reminded me so much of walking down the stairs with Miss Pricket when I was a little girl. I almost felt giddy. There was an excitement in the air. It was almost entirely dark, but I could hear the giggling of the housemaids, and Mrs. Baddeley shushing them as I was taken from the kitchen to the servants' hall. The scent of chocolate filled the air.

"What's going on? What's wrong with the lights?" I called out into the dark. And then, with a spark, they switched on.

"HAPPY BIRTHDAY, CRUELLA!"

Everyone was there. Jean, Paulie, the footmen, and Mrs. Baddeley. Within moments, Jackson joined us. My family. They were all there. "Oh, Anita! Did you arrange this?" She smiled and patted Mrs. Baddeley on the arm.

"Along with Mrs. Baddeley, and of course Jackson. They did all the work."

And they had gone all out. The room was beautifully decorated with black and white streamers and balloons. And sitting on the servants' hall table was the tallest, most elaborately decorated cake I had ever seen. "You've outdone yourself, Mrs. Baddeley!" It was a many tiered cake, with alternating dark chocolate and vanilla layers.

"I'm so happy you're all here," I said. "Especially you, Anita," I added in a low voice only she could hear.

"I have one more surprise for you, Cruella." Anita seemed very excited, and a little nervous. "I hope you won't mind." A familiar figure came out from the kitchen. It was Miss Pricket! But she looked different. She wasn't dressed like a governess. She was in a lovely little traveling suit, with matching shoes and handbag, and her hair was softly falling around her face.

"Miss Pricket!" I hadn't realized how much I had truly missed her. "I'm so happy to see you, Miss Pricket. Can you ever forgive me—" She stopped me before I could continue.

"Never mind that now, Cruella. I understand. I was just so happy when Anita wrote me to say you'd like to see me again." And I had. I had desperately wanted to see her again, but I'd feared she would reject me. I had told Anita about it in our many letters. Told her how I had felt after Christmas, how I felt I had made a terrible mistake. How I wished I could have changed everything after that horrible row with my mother on Christmas Eve. I told her how miserable I was, trapped at home with Mother without Anita or Miss Pricket to be my allies. And now Mother was gone, and I had my Anita and Miss Pricket back again. Life was good. It was as it should be.

It was a wonderful evening of merrymaking, the most fun I'd had in months. This time I didn't care if my mother came home or not. I neither wished for her to be there to help celebrate nor dreaded her return ruining our pretty time. Not that she would sully herself downstairs with the likes of Anita or the staff. Mother had completely slipped my mind. . . .

Until the bell rang—just like it had on Christmas Eve.

But this time, my heart didn't sink. I was eighteen. Mother no longer controlled me. And she had never controlled my money. According to the missive I'd received from our solicitors, my allowance was to be raised; I was to have an income of my own, and more control over the finances in general. The capital and house would still be held in trust until I was of age. Whatever she said to me when I opened that door, however she scolded me, it couldn't hurt me now.

But that bell would change my life more than I could ever have imagined. At the door was a gift. From my father. Arranged by him with his solicitor before his passing.

A gift for my eighteenth birthday.

I met Sir Huntley in the vestibule. He seemed surprised to find me coming from downstairs, but said nothing on the matter. He just smiled, his round little eyes turning into half-moons. Beside him, on the round table in the center of the entry-way, was a wicker basket. Something was wiggling under the red blanket within.

"Miss Cruella, your father asked that I give you this along with the other provisions that were detailed in the missive I sent you last week. I trust you understood everything?"

"Yes, Sir Huntley, but what is this?" I asked, looking at the basket.

"This, my dear, is Perdita. A gift from your father." He smiled and took a puppy from the basket. She was the most adorable thing I had ever laid eyes on.

"Perdita!" I swooned. A puppy. A black-and-white puppy. A Dalmatian puppy. She was beautiful. She had a vivid red bow tied around her neck with a tag that had her name printed upon it. *Perdita*. "But how? Why?"

"Your father made arrangements in his will that you were to be gifted Perdita on your eighteenth birthday. He was very specific on the breed and name."

"Isn't Perdita a character in *A Winter's Tale*?" I asked, wondering if Papa simply chose the name because he knew I was fond of such stories, or if there was a deeper meaning.

"He said you would recognize the name. He also

gave me a note to go along with his gift. He said you would understand."

*Distinguish yourself.*

And I did understand. I understood it completely.

It was the same message Mother had included with every gift she had ever given to me. But it all started with the fur coat, the one that nearly overshadowed the mysterious jade earrings Papa had given me. He must have seen her note that night in my room. *Distinguish yourself.* Her meaning was quite different than his, of course. She wanted me to be more like her. To distinguish myself from everyone else. But Papa had always wanted me to be my own woman. He wanted me to distinguish myself from my mother.

I felt like this was a sign that I was doing the right thing by distancing myself from my mother. I felt like he would approve of the choices I had made since he'd died.

"Your father always wanted to give you a puppy, Cruella. He was only sorry he had to wait until he was gone to do it," said Sir Huntley. "He said it was something you always asked for, but Lady De Vil resolutely forbade." That was true. I'd cried myself to sleep many nights when I was a girl, wishing I could have a puppy. A Dalmatian puppy, to be exact. And my papa remembered.

I loved my father more than ever in that moment. And I loved Perdita. I had Anita and Miss Pricket home with me again, and for the first time I didn't need my mother. I felt like all was right in my world.

And I couldn't have been more wrong.

## CHAPTER IX

# CRACKERJACK TIMING

Anita and I had a swanky evening planned for the night after my little birthday party with the servants. I almost couldn't stand the thought of leaving poor Perdita downstairs with the staff so Anita and I could go out to dinner. I knew she would be safe with Mrs. Baddeley and the others fussing over her, but I couldn't help worrying. Anita and Miss Pricket talked me into going out nevertheless.

"Oh, Cruella! Perdita will be treated like a little queen down in the kitchen. Mrs. Baddeley has been saving scraps of meat for her all day," said Miss Pricket.

"Please, it's your eighteenth birthday, Cruella.

We have to celebrate!" said Anita. Both of them implored me with their sweet smiles and puppy dog eyes.

"Well, if you're both going to gang up on me like this, I might regret my decision to have you stay with us for a while, Miss Pricket," I said, laughing. She knew I was joking. Miss Pricket and I had fallen into a new stride with each other since she had come back. All was well with us, as if nothing at all had happened. I tried talking with her about it, when I asked if she'd like to stay until her next engagement, which started in a few weeks. I felt I needed to tell her how sorry I was, but she wouldn't hear it. All she would say was that she understood and that Anita had explained everything. I really felt quite lucky to have Anita and Miss Pricket back again. I had almost written her so many times, but I poured all of my regrets and misgivings into my letters to Anita. She was the only person I could confide in, and I was so happy I had, because she took it upon herself to let Miss Pricket know how deeply sorry I really was.

As we were trying to decide what to wear for

our night out, I remembered I had a gift for Anita. "Miss Pricket, will you get me that big white box at the bottom of my closet?" The box had a big red ribbon with a tag that Miss Pricket read aloud.

"'Anita'!" she said as she brought the box over to her. Anita flushed.

"Oh, Cruella. What's this? It's your birthday, not mine."

I giggled like we were small girls again.

"Just open it, Anita. I hope I got the size right." Anita took her time opening the box, undoing the bow with small precise gestures.

"Anita! Open the damn thing! Come on! I'm excited for you to see it." She lifted the lid to reveal a pool of shimmering light blue and silver: a cocktail dress, one of those sparkling, slinky numbers. Anita's hand fluttered to her mouth.

"Oh, Cruella, it's beautiful. Thank you." I knew Anita's guardian didn't lavish his ward with gifts and expensive clothing the way he did his own daughters. And I didn't want her feeling out of place when we went out. This would be the first of many gifts I had planned to give Anita. Oh, I had such great plans for us. And I couldn't wait to share them with her at dinner.

"Cruella, do you want to wear the black and silver?" Miss Pricket asked. I did. It was my favorite dress. "Oh! And my black-and-white fur. And my jade earrings," I said.

Miss Pricket smiled at us and said, "You are both going to look so lovely tonight. I wish I could see it." Anita flinched, and I could see she thought I should have invited Miss Pricket to dinner with us. I almost thought I should. She was, after all, there as a friend, even though she had quite seamlessly stepped right back into the role of being my lady's maid. The last thing I wanted to do was make her uncomfortable. But I asked her nevertheless. I was a new woman, after all, and I was stepping out of the traditional lady's role. Why not invite her?

"Miss Pricket, you wouldn't want to join us this evening, would you?"

Miss Pricket smiled, tears almost coming to her

eyes. "Thank you, my dear, no. Though it means so much to me that you would ask, this is your special evening, and it's going to be magical."

❖ ❖ ❖ ❖

The restaurant was glittering. It was everything I had wanted and hoped for. It was the first time Anita and I had been out together without a chaperone. I was eighteen. And Miss Pricket agreed it would be acceptable if we had the evening to ourselves.

As we walked up to the maître d', I saw us in a large gilded mirror to our right. The words *distinguish yourself* rang in my ears as I looked at myself in the mirror. I felt empowered that evening wearing my finery, my coat and my earrings. I felt like I was on top of the world. And I had Anita at my side. I decided it was the perfect night to spring my news on her. My grand idea of touring the world together.

I knew she would be just as excited as I was. I waited until after dinner to tell her, and I was so giddy with anticipation Anita thought I'd had a bit too much sugar.

"Cruella! Maybe we should slow down a bit,"

she said, pulling the dessert plate closer to her. She always made me laugh.

"Anita, stop. I have some news!"

She smiled. "I have some news, too, but you tell me yours first!"

I slammed my hand down on the table dramatically and exclaimed: "You're going to be sprung from Miss Upturn's in just a couple months, and as soon as you are, I want us to travel the world together! Oh, Anita, let's start our adventure somewhere exotic— like Egypt! We can see the pyramids, ride camels. Or maybe we can find where my earrings are from, track down that pirate and see if he demands them back from me! Let's escape stuffy London society and its insipid rules. We can go anywhere."

Anita's smile faded. This was not what I was expecting. I'd thought she would be happy. I'd thought she would be excited. I'd thought she would be *thankful*.

"What's wrong? Do you want to go somewhere else? We can go anywhere you'd like! The world is ours to explore."

"Oh, Cruella," Anita said sadly. "I can't go. I'm going to typing school right after I graduate from Miss Upturn's."

"Typing school?" I couldn't think of anything duller. "Whatever for?"

"Cruella, I love learning French, how to paint, how to dance. I love all of it, but none of it will help me in the real world. I need a way to make a living for myself. I don't want to be a governess or a companion to a snooty lady." Her words stung. Was that what she thought of me?

"I see," I said.

"No! That's not what I meant." She was mortified. "You're different from the other ladies. I love you, you know I do, but Cruella, you don't know what it's like in the real world. You don't have to worry about money. I need skills that will earn me an income I can depend on."

"But Anita, I am offering to *show* you the real world! And you don't have to worry about money. I'll pay for everything."

"And what if you fall in love with someone?

What if your life takes you in another direction? Where will that leave me?"

"I won't meet someone! I don't want to marry. And I always want you with me! As my companion. I will always take care of you."

"So I'd be a servant."

"No, not a servant. My friend."

"Your friend who you pay to spend time with you." Anita reached across the table and took my hand sadly. "Oh, Cruella. I love you dearly, but don't you see? I need to make my own way for myself in the world. I'm so sorry to disappoint you." I drew my hand away, and Anita flinched.

"It's fine. I understand," I said. But I didn't understand. What was so great about typing school that was worth abandoning your best friend? I was hurt.

"Are we okay, Cruella? Are you cross with me?"

I said I wasn't, but I was terribly disappointed. The rest of the evening was very quiet between us. I didn't even ask her about her news. I assumed she was just going to tell me about typing school. I supposed she was very excited about it, if someone could be excited about such a thing.

That night, as I lay in bed, it occurred to me that with Anita going off to school, and my mother off on her travels, I was truly alone. I knew it was silly, but I had imagined that Anita and I would be friends forever. I hadn't thought there would ever be a day when she would really leave me. But I guess we were both growing up. Maybe her place was typing school. And she seemed to be pushing me in the same direction as my mother had: to marry some boring lord. All I wanted was to escape the stifling life my mother was trying to thrust upon me. And now Anita was sticking me in the same box.

Perdita snuggled up against me in bed, and I stroked her soft fur, wondering how it had all gone so terribly wrong, wondering why Anita didn't love me as I'd hoped she did. And wondering if I couldn't persuade Miss Pricket to stay with me. Because without Anita, I had no one.

The rest of Anita's visit was awkward. She spent

most of her time downstairs visiting with the servants, and I busied myself with the running of the household. Mama had written to say she was coming home. I was hoping Anita would be headed back to school before Mama returned, but Jackson received word she would be arriving that night—Anita's last night. We would have to suffer a quiet, strained dinner together. At least it was just for one night, and Anita would be gone the next morning. My mother could yell at me all she wanted then.

❖ ❖ ❖ ❖

The dining room table was set to perfection, and the room was almost overwhelmed by flowers and candles. I looked perfect. Something about putting on my old trappings made me feel like myself again. And it made me miss my mama. Especially now that Anita was leaving me.

I'd decided to give my mama a grand welcome. I wanted us to be friends again. And I wanted everything to go perfectly. If only Anita hadn't been there, but it couldn't be helped. At that point I was just terribly disappointed with her. And she, too, seemed disappointed with me. Things felt different between us. Only now, in retrospect, do I see our friendship really ended the night she refused to travel the world with me. The night she picked a mundane life over one of adventure, with me.

In my mind, preparing for my mama's return was just as important as having the Queen to dinner. I made sure to dress impeccably, taking care to wear Papa's jade earrings and one of my loveliest dresses. I had the servants working all day to make sure the dining room was perfectly decorated, and the menu featured all of my mama's favorites. Jackson had advised me that there would be an extra guest for dinner, a guest of my mama's. I was curious who she would be bringing with her, but I was happy for the extra guest, so it wouldn't just be me, Mama, and Anita. One thing I learned at Miss Upturn's is that even numbers at dinner are always better.

Anita and I were in the morning room when Mama walked in. Following behind her was an exquisitely handsome man. He was older than me by a handful of years. Still, he was youthful, and decidedly American. He didn't have that stuffiness that the men in London pride themselves on. And he wasn't afraid to show his emotions or say what was on his mind.

"Cruella, my dear," my mother said, by way of greeting me for the first time in weeks, "this is Lord Shortbottom. I met him on my travels, and then quite by chance we were on the same return ship to London. I knew at once he was someone you had to meet, and I just had to invite him to dinner, especially after he told me he would otherwise be dining alone at his club this evening. I was sure you wouldn't mind."

"I don't mind at all. Welcome to our home, Lord Shortbottom—" But the brazen man interrupted me.

"Please, do call me Jack. I've been telling your mother to do the same, but she always insists on formalities. I do hope you won't be scandalized by my unconventional ways, Lady Cruella."

"Indeed not, Jack," I said, taking a good look at him before I introduced him to Anita. "And please let me introduce you to my dear friend Anita. We've been friends since we were girls together."

Jack made a great show of going to Anita and kissing her hand. "Enchanted, my dear. Simply enchanted." But his eyes were on me. Jack was almost too slick, too charming, and I wondered how it was that he'd befriended my mother. He wasn't her sort. Clearly he had money enough, but his breeding and lordship were in question. Jackson poured us drinks before dinner. We sat in the morning room sipping them while we waited for the gong. All the while I studied Jack as he told us of his travels and adventures around the world. I found I couldn't tear my eyes away from him. I was mesmerized by Jack already. He had a place in my heart almost the moment I laid eyes on him.

Through our conversations it became clear Jack had a fortune of his own, and a great deal more he was coming into. It was a great relief to hear of his many estates, here and in America, because then I knew his flirtations with me weren't about trying to get his hands on my money. And as for the question of his lordship, well, he was some distant cousin or another of a baronet who didn't have an heir to inherit, so everything was left to Jack. And suddenly I understood how this American got his handle. But the name Lord Shortbottom sounded ridiculous. I giggled to myself just thinking of it, happy he'd suggested I call him Jack.

Dinner was much livelier than I had imagined it would be. Mama directed the conversation to Jack whenever possible. She took pains to also include Anita when she could, and asked us about my birthday and our time together. In spite of the recent awkwardness with Anita, I was so happy Mama was making an effort with her. She knew how important she was to me, and I had been dreading to see how she would behave. I'd thought Mama would be angry she was there. It gave me hope that my mother was as eager as I was to mend our relationship.

"We had a lovely party for Cruella downstairs," Anita said. I glanced at her sharply and realized she was trying to get a rise out of my mother. She had been that way since our debacle of a dinner, snippy and rude, and impatient with me. Mama's eyes almost popped out of her head with anger, but Jack took it all in stride.

"Well, isn't that a scream?" he said. "I've heard stories about old families and their relationships with their servants, and I think it's quaint."

"You come from a very old family, Lord Shortbottom, though growing up an American I can see how your experience might be very different," said my mother, composing herself and trying to change the subject. I didn't understand why Anita was trying to ruin our evening. Why would she say something she knew would anger my mother? Especially since she knew I was clearly trying to make amends with her.

"Oh, I think I fancied my cook, like most children did growing up in houses like these. She was like a second mother to me, really. Doting on me, sending me all my favorites when I was away at boarding school. Scolding me when my boots got muddy, but then turning around and arranging some little celebration in the kitchen for me on special days. So I would have something a little less formal and homier. I'm guessing you love your cook as much as I loved mine."

"Oh yes, Cruella adores Mrs. Baddeley. She is also like a second mother, to both of us," said Anita, needling my mama again for some reason.

"I do adore her," I said, kicking Anita under the table, hoping it would make her stop with these provocative comments.

"Why, Mrs. Baddeley is the only person Cruella would trust to care for her sweet Perdita, aside from me."

Blast! I hadn't told Mama about Perdita yet.

"Perdita? Who is Perdita?" my mother asked.

"My puppy. We can talk about it after dinner, Mama," I said, shooting a look at Anita and kicking her again. Harder this time. And then I added, "Should the ladies withdraw to the drawing room?"

Thank goodness Jackson intervened, saving us from an uncomfortable conversation in front of our guest. "Would the gentleman like some port before he joins the ladies in the drawing room?"

"Yes, I would, Jackson." Jack gave him a wide Clark Gable smile. A smile I was already growing to love and adore. A smile that reminded me of someone. Someone I loved and missed terribly.

We ladies went into the drawing room, knowing we didn't have much time before Jack would join us. I didn't want to discuss Perdita that evening. I was angry with Anita for bringing her up at dinner. Honestly, I was completely taken aback by Anita's attitude in general.

"Mama, I wanted to wait until later to tell you about Perdita. She's a dear creature. And a gift from Papa. He meant to give her to me on my eighteenth birthday." My mother flinched at the mention of Papa.

"What do you mean, Cruella? What are you saying?"

Anita could see I was struggling for words. Perhaps she felt guilty for being such a little twit at dinner. I didn't know, but she tried to put her finishing school lessons to good use and change the direction of the conversation.

"How was your trip, Lady De Vil? I would so love to see America. Is it as wild and untamed as everyone says?"

But my mother didn't lose a beat. She kept her eyes and questions fixed on me.

"Speaking of wild and untamed. Tell me how it was your father gave you a puppy, Cruella, considering he's no longer with us?" She sipped the brandy Jackson had just poured for her, looking at both Anita and me like she might eat us whole. I suddenly felt very small. Like a little girl, afraid of my mother. She seemed like a wild beast contemplating her prey.

"Well, Mama, he arranged it with Sir Huntley before he died." I hated how small my voice sounded.

"Clearly he arranged it before he died, Cruella. I didn't imagine he rose from the grave to bestow puppies. But why on earth would you accept such a gift? And what possessed him to give you such a thing? Your father knew how I felt about animals, Cruella. He knew I didn't want them in the house. We discussed it countless times while you were growing up. Always wanting to get you a puppy. Well, I suppose this was his way of getting the last word!"

"I suppose that would be the only way he could, Lady De Vil," Anita said, smiling at my mother.

"Anita!" I blurted. "Stop needling my mama! This behavior of yours is becoming tiresome."

I couldn't stand the way Anita was acting. She was ruining everything. All I wanted was a lovely evening with my mama. A chance to be friends again. But Anita was taking every opportunity she could to make her angry with me.

"Mama, I adore Perdita. Please, won't you give her a chance? She's an adorable little creature."

"Cruella, I was hoping to spend more time at home with you. But if we're going to have a puppy running around the house, I don't see how that will be possible. I hate the creatures. Dirty, nasty things that they are. The only good thing about them is their fur! Now, if we made a nice muffler out of her to match my coat, then she would be useful." Anita squeaked with fright and my jaw dropped in shock.

"Mama!" But before we could continue the conversation, Jack came into the room.

"Jack, hello! Just in time," Mama said, smiling at him. The conversation quickly shifted back to Jack, and Mama directed it toward his many estates, his fortune, and his desire to find a wife to share his life with. She was clearly very keen on my marrying him. And I was starting to feel as if I wouldn't fight her on it. I liked him. Both Mama and Anita were being beasts, and here, almost like magic, an exceptional man was plopped into my lap, possessing almost every quality I could possibly wish for. However, it was far too soon to be talking of such things.

But my mother kept pressing.

"So, Lord Shortbottom, I'm sure you're eager to marry. A man of your status is probably eager to have an heir. Someone to continue your name. Someone to leave your fortune to. And you seem to have caught my Cruella's eye. I wonder if we won't be hearing wedding bells in the near future. My daughter is someone who does seem to get whatever she wants."

"Mama!" I was scandalized. She knew I couldn't take my husband's name. And it was far too soon to be pressuring Jack into the notion of marriage.

"Oh, Cruella. You can't deny I've been parading men past you for months now and you've not looked at a single one with interest. And in one evening you're enchanted by Lord Shortbottom. Of course marriage is going to spring to mind, my dear. You can't fault your dear mama for wanting the best for her favorite girl," she continued, with a large grin on her face. "Lord and Lady Shortbottom. It has a ring to it, don't you think?" I couldn't believe my mother was acting this way. I was thoroughly mortified.

"Mother, you know that isn't possible, and really, it isn't the time to discuss this. Please, Mama. You're making everyone most uncomfortable."

"Please don't censor yourself on my account, ladies. It's refreshing to have a real conversation in an English drawing room. And since we are talking candidly, let me just say I would be the happiest man alive if your daughter agreed to let me court her. I am already completely besotted by her."

I remember blushing. This wasn't the first of this kind of conversation I'd had in my mother's drawing room. But it was the first time I'd blushed.

"Well, Jack," I said, still trying his name on for size, "even if I were to let a man court me, let alone marry him, my mother knows I cannot take my future husband's name. It's a condition in my father's will. I am the last of the De Vil line, you see, and it was his wish I carry on his name. I'm sorry she misled you."

"Well, I never really cared for my name. Lord Jack De Vil sounds a heck of a lot better than Lord Shortbottom," he said, laughing. "Don't you think?" And I did. I thought it sounded very well indeed. And I couldn't have been happier to hear it. But the mood shifted in the room after his declaration. Perhaps Mama had too much to drink, or she was exhausted by Anita's behavior, or the news of Perdita, or all of it, but she spiraled into one of her dark and brooding moods. The sort that would likely have her in her room for days, complaining of a headache. The evening ended on such a strange note, but not before Jack and I said our goodbyes in the drawing room. Mama had invented a reason to usher Anita out of the room, leaving us to part on our own.

"It was lovely meeting you, Jack," I said, feeling so awkward about how the evening went, yet so thrilled to have finally met a man who captured my imagination.

"I hope I will be able to see you again," he said. I shouldn't have been surprised that he just came out and said it. He was such a direct man. So unlike the other men I was used to, endlessly talking around subjects.

"Will you be in London again soon?" I asked.

"If it meant I got to see you." He flashed me one of his magic movie-star smiles.

"You're not at all like the men I'm used to," I said, almost blushing again.

"I hope that's a compliment, Cruella. Should I invent a reason to come to London again?"

He always made me laugh, even from that very first night.

"It is the highest compliment. And I'd like it very much if you came to see me again, Jack," I said, making him smile again.

"I know it's early days, Cruella, but I know you feel the connection between us. You don't seem to be a lady who suffers fools. Tell me I haven't been foolish this evening."

I looked at him, realizing I could fall in love with him—if I hadn't already. "No, Jack, the very last thing I would call you is a fool." And with that, he kissed me lightly on the cheek and wished me a good night.

All of this probably sounds foolish . . . unless you have fallen in love. If you have been lucky enough to have love hit you like a lightning bolt then you don't need any convincing. It was as if my dear, sweet departed papa had tapped my mama on the shoulder and whispered in her ear to bring this man home to me. He was absolutely everything I wanted. The exception to my rule.

After Jack left, I replayed the evening over and over in my head, wondering why Mama and I spoke so candidly with him. Perhaps Jack's cavalier American style was rubbing off on us already. I didn't know. But what I did know was there was something between Jack and me. Something I had never expected to happen. For the first time, I was actually contemplating marriage.

But Anita had other notions.

## CHAPTER X

# GOODBYE, PERDITA

After Jack left and my mother went sulking to her room, Anita and I stayed up chatting in my bedroom before we went to sleep. Anita had Paulie bring Perdita up to my room, and the three of us sat on my bed together. But no matter how cute and cuddly Perdita was, she couldn't wipe the scowl from Anita's face. I thought she was sour about having to go back to school the next day. Or perhaps she was regretting her decision to go to typing school rather than travel the world with me. I wondered if she thought I would wait around forever for her to change her mind. It was quite possible she'd seen her chance fly out the window when she saw how much I fancied Jack. But if anyone should've been feeling sour, it was me. Anita had acted horribly at dinner, and quite possibly ruined my chances at fixing things with my mama.

"Anita, what's wrong with you? Why were you acting that way at dinner, needling my mama like that?"

"You see what she's doing, don't you?" she asked, making a pretense of playing with Perdita, though her gaze was fixed on me.

"What exactly do you think she's doing, Anita?" I was losing patience with her. Honestly, I was starting to feel glad she was leaving the next day.

"She's trying to marry you off. Even you can see that, Cruella," she said, clearly trying to tick me off. I wasn't going to take the bait.

"It's no secret she wants to see me married. This isn't news, Anita. She's been parading me around all year. Besides, all mothers want to see their daughters married."

"But does she have to be so mercenary?" she said, rolling her eyes.

"Mothers have been hunting men with fortunes for their daughters since the beginning of time, Anita. You're a fool if you think my mother is any different. It's her job."

"Cruella, she's clearly trying to get her hands on your fortune. Look how she made such a point of saying your name would be Shortbottom." This time she had crossed the line. I was truly angry with her.

"You'd better take that back, Anita! That isn't true. You have the wrong end of the stick!"

"I don't think I do. I thought even *you* would see through your mother's sudden interest in spending time at home, Cruella. And that comment about making Perdita into a muffler was horrifying."

"Clearly you don't have a high opinion of my mama if you think she was serious. And what do you mean that *even I* can see what she's up to?"

"Oh, Cruella, I've been waiting for you to see her clearly for years. And I thought you did after the scene she made at Christmas. I've put up with your snobbish attitude for a long time because I love you, and because I knew in my heart that wasn't who you really are. And you proved it at Christmas, when you started treating your staff like a family, and stopped, well, acting like your mother. I thought I had my old Cruella back. And now she's home for one evening, and you're back to acting like her. Defending her. It's sad, Cruella."

"You're just upset that I've met someone! You're jealous!" I said, getting up from the bed. And I was sure I was right. Anita had been acting strange ever since I'd asked her to travel the world with me, but once she met Jack, she'd started acting like an insolent little brat.

"Jealous of a man you just met?" She laughed. "Cruella, please think about this clearly just for one moment. This isn't about Jack. It's about you and your mother."

"I do think it's about Jack. He's a remarkable man, Anita. Did you ever stop to think that I might actually really like him? Or that my choosing a life with him, on my own terms, pushes my mother even further away from me? I never thought I would meet a man like him, Anita. Never! He's everything I've ever wanted or wished for. He's exactly the sort of man Papa would have wanted for me. And if you can't see that, well, then you don't know me as well as I thought you did. I think this is about you regretting your decision, choosing a mundane life over the life you could have had with me. That's what I think this is about, Anita."

"Oh, Cruella. He's funny and charming, yes, and a bit like your father. They have the same smile. But you hardly know him. Don't let your mother manipulate you like this. Forcing you into marriage and out of your inheritance."

"You heard him. He doesn't mind taking my name," I said. Looking back, I don't even know why I was trying to defend myself or my mother to an in-between like Anita. Why it was so important to me that she believed me. I suppose I still loved her.

"Why were you even talking about marriage? You just met him, Cruella. You have so many plans for yourself. You wanted to travel the world. You said you would never marry, and now in one evening everything has changed. It doesn't make sense. It's like your mother has some sort of hold on you, Cruella. You've been acting so strangely lately. Like wearing the furs she gave you somehow makes you act like her."

I laughed. "That's nonsense, Anita. By your logic, then, wearing the earrings my father gave me would make me act like him? None of this makes sense. My mother isn't trying to control me. And she isn't trying to take my fortune. It's insulting."

"Cruella, you saw how your mother reacted when she found out he was willing to keep the De Vil name! I don't think she counted on Lord Shortbottom relinquishing his name so easily. He's thwarted her plans, Cruella. And now she's threatening you with leaving again if you keep Perdita. She's trying to erase your father. His gifts to you, and his name!"

"I won't give up my father's name, Anita. I promised I wouldn't."

"Because you love your father, or because you love his money?" Anita was getting angrier by the moment. I couldn't understand how she could have gotten it all so wrong. Neither of us were paying attention to Perdita, so the little *beast* acted out in the only way she knew how to get our attention. She peed on my fur coat! Can you believe it?

I'd had it. "Get out of my room, Anita. And take that *mongrel* with you!"

"Mongrel? What's wrong with you? She's your sweet puppy and she's just nervous because we were arguing, Cruella." I couldn't believe she was defending the wicked creature.

"Bloody dog!" I said, ringing the bell. "Now the maid will have to get my coat cleaned! Hopefully it's not ruined."

*"The maid?* Her name is Jean, Cruella! Do you hear yourself?"

"I don't care what her name is as long as she saves that coat! Now get that beast out of here! Take her downstairs, and be quiet about it. I don't want my mama seeing the little menace upstairs."

I remember seeing the sad look on Anita's face when she left the room with Perdita. She looked heartbroken. I was heartbroken, too. I couldn't believe what she'd said about my mama. To think Mama was scheming to take my money. The entire idea was scandalous, and beneath my mother. Beneath her dignity. Hunting down a man, bringing him home to meet me with the hopes I would take his name so Papa's money would revert to her. It was out of the realm of possibility. I wouldn't believe it.

✤ ✤ ✤ ✤

Anita and Perdita were gone the next morning. Even though I was angry with her, part of me was sad to see Anita go. I was still stinging over the things she'd said about Mama, and still hurt she wouldn't travel the world with me. I still loved her. But I was happy she was gone. And I was relieved she was able to take Perdita with her. As much as I cherished Papa's gift, I knew that if I wanted to have a friendship with my mama I couldn't keep her. My papa was gone. There was nothing I could do to bring him back. But if I wanted my mama in my life I had to do something to make her happy, to make her love me again, and the only thing I could think of was to get rid of Anita and Perdita. It broke my heart to see Perdita go, but I wasn't going to let anything stand in the way of my relationship with my mama. Not an in-between like Anita, and *certainly* not a puppy.

## CHAPTER XI

# TICKTOCK

After that, Anita and I wrote to each other less frequently. I used Perdita as an excuse to check in from time to time to see how she was faring. Anita's letters made it clear she had made a cock-up of her life, just as I expected.

Of course, *she* didn't see it that way. She was quite happy, or at least said so in her letters to me over the years. She went to typing school just as she'd planned and found herself a little flat near a park where she spent her idle time with Perdita, who by all accounts was thriving in Anita's care. Most of our correspondences were about Perdita, with little bits of news of our own lives peppered throughout our missives. Anita eventually met that jingle-writing fool Roger, when his Dalmatian got his leash tangled with Perdita's at the park. Can you believe it? How disgustingly adorable.

The two of them now lived in poverty with only one servant to speak of, who I could only imagine was a dumpy-looking woman, old enough to be Anita's grandmother. Of course, that's not how Anita described her. She said she was a sweet, older, and very jolly woman. Well, if that doesn't sound like a dumpy old woman, then I really don't know what would.

Besides, I honestly didn't have much time to devote to thinking about Anita, her idiot musician, and their pair of spotted beasts. I was too busy living the life of luxury with Jack. Whatever had happened the night Mama brought him to dinner couldn't have been all that bad, because he called on me the very next day. It wasn't long before we became an item, and his arrival in my life just as Anita left it felt quite written in the stars.

Let me tell you about Jack. My Crackerjack!

Oh, he was a handsome devil! Even more handsome than the leading men in films. He was the love of my life, and it wasn't too long before he was my husband as well.

Jack De Vil!

Yes, duckies, that's right, he took my name, just as he said he would. And I never thought less of him for it. All my ideas of a man not willing to take his wife's name flew right out the window when I met Jack.

Jack joined me on my travels instead of Anita. Oh, the adventures we had together! The places we saw. The glamorous life we led. His personality could fill an entire room, so I am sure you can imagine what we were like together. We were the *it* couple. Always dressed to kill, always making it into the papers. Always the funniest and smartest couple at any event. We were a force of nature. It was as if Anita leaving my life changed it for the better. I was becoming the woman I was meant to be.

I was Cruella De Vil! The heiress. The lady of the manor.

And I was living my life exactly how I wanted.

I suppose you want to hear about my wedding day. Oh, but I'm so eager to jump ahead to the events that have brought me to Hell Hall, where I am now. And I want so much to share my latest plans with you. But I mustn't skip any of my story, and what is my story without my Crackerjack?

Of course, he (and Mama) arranged the most magnificent wedding imaginable. It was a glittering affair. And Jack, well, he insisted on paying for all of it. He was sweet that way, my Jack. Always wanting to make people happy. Always showing them he loved them. And oh, how he loved me. Our wedding rivaled the royal weddings. To be honest, I do think if it was within his power he would have crowned me queen. But he did manage to make me feel like one, and not only on our wedding day. He did so for the entirety of our marriage, right up until the end. He did everything he could to ensure my happiness, from suggesting I keep Miss Pricket on as my lady's maid to helping me make amends with my mama, and encouraging me to invite Anita to the wedding. He even helped me see where I went wrong with her.

He often suggested reconnecting with Anita, but I couldn't bring myself to betray my mama in that way. I could never forget all those horrible things she'd said. Writing to Anita on occasion didn't feel like betrayal, but seeing her, bringing her into my home, I felt would be the ruin of everything. Ever since I decided to marry Jack, life was magical with my mama. She had a purpose. Something to focus on. And for the first time, *I* was her focus. She helped Jack and me with all the wedding preparations. Of course Jack wouldn't let her pay for a thing, but he let her have a say in all the planning, which made her sublimely happy.

We decided to make the rehearsal dinner a small affair. Just Jack, Mama, and myself. We had it at home, and Mama arranged for a lovely evening. The dining room was filled with candles and flowers. Sitting around that table where I'd had so many dinners with Anita, I have to admit I missed her that night. I wished she were there. My heart hadn't hardened completely to Anita. There was still a soft spot for her even then. But I couldn't bring myself to invite her to the wedding, let alone the rehearsal dinner, even if I did feel her absence keenly. Even though I was nervous about the idea of talking with Anita again, and worried it would ruin things with Mama if I did, there was an empty space in my heart reserved for Anita.

It was going to be my last evening as an unmarried woman. Though I hadn't been the sort of girl who daydreamed about the night before my wedding, the evening wasn't as I had imagined. I'd always thought I would spend it with Anita.

"What's the matter, my darling?" Jack took my hand. "You should be happy. What has you so vexed?"

"Nothing, Jack. It's nothing. I am exceedingly happy. I promise you," I said, but he wasn't convinced.

"I can't have my Cruella sad the night before her wedding. I know what's the matter. You regret not inviting Anita."

"I suppose I do," I said.

"Oh, Cruella. Don't give that girl another thought," said my mama. But Jack didn't agree.

"I say you call her. Call her this moment and tell her you want her there. Hell, tell her you want her in the wedding! I made sure Miss Pricket arranged a dress for her in case you changed your mind. Do it now, my love. Do it before you lose your nerve." He was really quite convincing, my Jack. His smile always won me over.

"Do you really think she would come?" I was so excited. Jack's goodwill and optimism were infectious.

"I do think she would come, my love. Now skedaddle and make that call."

"I think I will!" I said as Jackson came into the room to see if Jack would like to sit in the dining room with his port while we ladies went into the drawing room.

"Yes, Jackson. I will sit in here for a spell while Cruella makes her call. Can you arrange a line for her in the sitting room? She would like to call

Miss Anita," he said. Then he gave me a big kiss right in front of Mama. (Americans. You have to love their audacity.) Mama and I left Jack to his port, and I poured Mama and myself some tea. I waited for Jackson to come back and arrange my call to Anita.

"Cruella," Mama said, with clear disdain, "do you really think it's wise to invite Anita at the last moment? Don't you think she would be insulted that you hadn't invited her months ago along with the other guests?"

"Anita doesn't care about those sorts of things, Mama."

"Well then, perhaps you should think about how I would feel. It's bad enough I am losing my only daughter. Do I have to share the day not only with her husband but with an insolent girl who treated me with such disrespect in my own home? Would you insult me like that, Cruella? Would you do that to us, now that we've become such good friends again? You know how I detest that girl. Isn't it enough that I've allowed that Miss Pricket back into our household? Am I expected to suffer her company as well as Anita's?"

"Mama, Miss Pricket has been well out of your way. The poor thing has been hidden away and out of your sight. And besides, she is joining my household. After this evening she won't be spending another night under your roof. As far as Anita is concerned, though, you're right. I'm sorry, Mama. Jack is just trying to make me happy."

"What's that, love? Do I feel my ears burning? Were you talking about me?" Jack said as he came striding into the room, all smiles, with a little skip in his step.

"That was quick," I said.

"I couldn't stand to be parted from you one more moment! It's bad enough I have to go to my club this evening, and I won't see you until tomorrow at the wedding." My Jack was always so sweet like that. And don't get the wrong end of the stick, he always meant what he said. He was entirely devoted to me. "My dearest, if you don't mind, I think we will do away with this nonsense of men staying in the dining room to drink port while the ladies withdraw to the drawing room in our new home together. It's antiquated, and most of our lady friends can talk circles around most men anyway," he said, sitting on the love seat next to me.

"It's all the fashion, having the ladies and gentlemen withdraw to the same room. It's more lively, and modern."

"So, how did your call with Anita go?" he asked.

"Oh, well, Mama brought up a very good point. She thinks Anita would be insulted if I were to invite her at the last moment." Jack narrowed his eyes. I could tell what he was thinking, but he was too polite to say so in front of my mama.

"As you wish, my love," he said. "As long as you're happy." He flashed me his brilliant smile.

"I am, my love. Very happy. Perhaps I will call Anita when we get back from our honeymoon," I said. And I meant it. I honestly wanted her there for my wedding more than anything, but I couldn't upset Mama. I didn't want to ruin my new relationship with her.

"We should have her and her musician come stay with us, it will be a scream," Jack said. "It will be just the sort of thing we will need once we get back from all our travels, don't you think, dear? I can have some of my friends out as well. It will be the perfect opportunity for our friends to mingle and get to know each other."

"That sounds divine," I said, but I was distracted by Mama's frown. Jack kept talking.

"You know, I have half a mind to call Anita myself and tell her to come tomorrow. I know you won't truly be happy tomorrow unless she is there. I don't think we should wait until we're back from our travels."

Mama cleared her throat.

"Well, it seems like you have your life all figured out, Cruella. Since it doesn't seem as if you've factored me in at all, I suppose I should arrange to leave first thing tomorrow."

"Leave? First thing tomorrow? Mama! Tomorrow is my wedding."

"Yes, dear, but it can't be helped. I think it's

best if I were to leave for my trip sooner." I was in shock.

"What trip? You hadn't mentioned a trip before now."

"Come now, Lady De Vil. That isn't fair," said Jack, but I squeezed his hand, signaling him to leave it to me. I had an idea—maybe my last and only chance to get Mama to stay.

"Well, Mama, if you leave tomorrow then you will miss our big surprise, won't she, Jack?" Of course he had no idea what I was talking about, but he was a sharp one, my Jack, and he went along with it.

"Yes, my dear, she will," he said, giving me a look that said he wondered what I was up to.

"Well, Mama, Jack and I have been talking about this, and we've decided to sign over my inheritance."

"Oh, Cruella! Are you sure?" Mama asked. Her entire demeanor changed. She went from sulking and angry to looking quite jubilant in an instant.

"Of course we're sure," said Jack. "We have more money than we could possibly need for many lifetimes over." Oh, how I loved my Jack. We hadn't, of course, talked about this, but I knew he wouldn't mind.

"Yes, Mama. What's my fortune compared to Jack's? We don't need it, but you do! It makes sense. I so wanted to surprise you with the news after we got home from our honeymoon. All that's left is to let Sir Huntley know so he can bring over the paperwork for us to sign."

"Oh, Cruella! I love you!" she said, giving me the biggest kiss on the cheek. I didn't think I recalled her ever saying that to me. Not with words. It was the happiest day of my life. My mama finally knew how much I loved her. I was finally able to give her something she truly wanted.

Later, when we were alone saying our goodbyes before Jack went off to his club, he said, "Are you sure about this, my dear? Signing your entire estate over to your mother is a big decision. You know I don't mind. I'm just concerned you're doing this for

the wrong reasons." He was so sweet. Always looking out for me.

"What better reason is there, Jack, than to make
Mama happy? We don't need my father's money.
You said so yourself. I really want to do this for my
mama. It's important to me. And I'm still keeping
Papa's name. I'm still honoring his memory. It's the
perfect solution. And my darling, please don't call
Anita and have her come tomorrow. I don't want to
do anything to upset Mama. She's so happy."

"As long as *you're* happy, my love, I'm happy. But
if there is any hint of you pining for Anita when we
get back from our honeymoon then I will have to
insist you call her."

"Deal!" I said, but I had no intention of calling
her. I wasn't going to do anything to ruin my relationship with my mama. Not now, after I had finally
won her love.

## CHAPTER XII

# SIR HUNTLEY'S
# RESERVATIONS

Once Jack and I were back from our honeymoon in Venice and settled into our new home, I decided the first thing we should do was settle the question of signing my inheritance over to Mama. She had been so sweet during our entire trip, writing me letters telling me she couldn't wait for me to come home. Telling me how happy she was to have such a successful and wonderful daughter. Miss Pricket, who came along on our trip as my lady's maid, kept her comments to herself. I could see she didn't trust Mama, and it was quite clear Jack didn't, either, but I wanted to do this for her, and he was happy to go along with anything that would make me happy. What was it going to hurt giving her what, frankly, my father should have left to her in the first place?

The day after we arrived home we asked Sir Huntley to come over to discuss the details. Mama was out having tea with Lady Slaptton and would be coming over later for dinner so we could all sign the paperwork. It would be the first time I would have anyone in my new home, and I was brimming with excitement. Miss Pricket was taking care of organizing our new household staff and managed to get in quick introductions amid the preparations. So quick was my introduction that I couldn't remember anyone's name! I would have to rely on Miss Pricket to remind me later. I had more important matters to deal with. I knew Miss Pricket would make sure everything for the dinner with Mama would go beautifully. But first was the matter of Sir Huntley.

Jack and I sat in the study of our stately new home while waiting for Sir Huntley to arrive.

"Do you want me here when you talk to Sir Huntley, my dear? Or shall I leave you two alone?"

"Oh, I want you here, my Crackerjack," I said with a kiss.

"Well, this is your matter, my darling. I know you've quite made up your mind. I'll simply be here for moral support. Not that you'll need it," he said, looking even more dashing than Humphrey Bogart.

And before we knew it, Miss Pricket came into the room.

"Lord and Lady De Vil, Sir Huntley is here." She wore a disapproving look on her face. Miss Pricket didn't say outright that she disagreed with my plan, but she took no pains to hide how she felt. I found myself putting up with Miss Pricket's little comments and looks after Anita and I parted ways. I missed having an in-between who I considered a friend and companion. And Jack said it did me good to have a servant who could be frank with me from time to time. He said it kept me on my toes, whatever that meant. So I put up with her. After all, she made me feel like I was bringing a bit of my childhood home with me to my new home with Jack.

"Thank you, Miss Pricket," I said. "Please show

him in." I could see Sir Huntley's eyes widen as he entered the room. He was impressed with my new home. I should have met him in the grand vestibule to see his eyes pop out of his head. My new vestibule could've fit the entire main floor of Mama's place on Belgrave Square. The floors were made entirely of marble, and the room was simply bursting with roman statues. And the grand staircase, well, that was a marvel. I couldn't wait to show it all off to Mama later when she came for dinner.

"Hello, Sir Huntley. Welcome to my new home. Miss Pricket, can you have the maid please bring in our tea?"

The staff in my new home was enormous. There was no way I was going to remember all of their names. So I took to calling them by their job titles when talking to Miss Pricket, and calling them "dear" when speaking to them directly. I left the remembering of names to Miss Pricket, who had taken on the role of head housekeeper. She directed the maid to bring in the tea, serving Sir Huntley first. He sipped his tea nervously as I shared my wishes for my father's money with him. Jack simply sat there beside me, flashing his wide Clark Gable smile, listening but not interjecting. Jack wasn't the sort of husband who felt he had to do the talking for his wife. He valued my mind, my sharp wit, and my sometimes wicked tongue.

"Lady De Vil, it is my duty as your solicitor to say this is very ill-advised. Your father wouldn't have wanted you to sign all of your money over to your mother."

"What does the money matter to me, Sir Huntley? I am very well taken care of by Jack. Why shouldn't Mama have the money? Papa should have left it to her in the first place."

"Your father wanted you to have something of your own. He wanted you to be your own person. To distinguish yourself."

"And so I have! And I've kept his name. What does it matter if I give Mama his money?"

"He was very clear on that point, Lady De Vil. He asked me to avoid it at all costs."

"But why was he so dead set against Mama

having the money? I've married a man with a fortune far greater than my own. It would be selfish to keep my father's money for myself when I can give it to my poor mama."

"Your mother draws a very sizable income from your capital holdings, Cruella. She is by no means poor. I'm sorry to have to say so . . ." he said, trailing off as he tried to find the right words.

"Please, Sir Huntley, speak as candidly as you like. You won't offend us," I said.

"Thank you, Lady De Vil, I didn't want to bring this up, but your father was afraid that if the capital was left in her charge, she would squander it, leaving you with nothing when she passed. That's why he left it to you."

I looked at my Jack, trying to read his face. I didn't want him thinking less of my mama. But his face was passive.

Sir Huntley looked as if he had more to say but was trying very hard to arrive at the right words without offending me. But then he found his courage.

"Your mother's spending is frankly outrageous, even for a woman of her means. She refuses to take advice on the matter, and has been working tirelessly to seize control over the trust since your father passed. I made a promise to your father, Lady De Vil, to protect you. And protect you I shall." Sir Huntley was by nature a nervous man, but I had never seen him so rattled. He was clearly very devoted to my father and intended to do all he could to stay true to his word. But I wasn't going to listen to this sort of talk about my mother, not for one more moment. *Working tirelessly to seize my money? Ever since my father died?* It didn't seem possible.

"I don't believe it. I won't have you telling such lies about my mother, sir!"

"I assure you it's true, Lady De Vil. I have a note here written in your mother's hand stating her intentions to have you married to Lord Shortbottom. . . ." The poor man's hands were shaking. I wanted to put him out of his misery, but I think I sort of enjoyed seeing him so wound up. "I'm sorry, I meant *Lord De Vil,*" he said, looking at Jack.

"Please, do call me Jack," Jack said, smiling over his cup of tea and trying to cut the tension in the room. Oh, my Jack. Always trying to fix everything with a smile.

"Yes. I'm sorry," said the round-faced man, clearly ruffled. "Please." He handed me the letter. "Read it for yourself."

It was just a folded piece of paper. A harmless thing. But it seemed ominous to me. Deadly. And I didn't want to touch it.

"Darling, Jack. Will you read it?" I asked.

"Yes, my dear," he said, taking the letter from the nervous solicitor. "Shall I read it aloud?" I couldn't believe I was so nervous. That a small folded piece of paper could elicit such terror.

"No, just read it. We will discuss it later."

I could see the color in my husband's face fade away as he read the letter, only for a moment, as if a deep and penetrating sadness washed over him. He composed himself quickly, put the letter in his breast pocket, and took my hand. "My sweetest dear," he said, with the saddest look on his face. He didn't have to tell me Sir Huntley was right. He didn't have to tell me what the letter said. Everyone was right about my mother. My father, Sir Huntley, Miss Pricket, and quite possibly Anita. But it was no matter. Why shouldn't she be hurt by my father leaving all his money to me? Why shouldn't she want me to marry a rich man? Did that make her an evil person? I thought not. And I couldn't stand the look on Jack's face. I never wanted to see pity in his eyes when looking at me. Not ever again.

"It's no matter. I would still like her to have the money," I said. I had made up my mind.

"But Lady De Vil!" Even Sir Huntley's bulldog jowls seemed to jiggle in protest.

"You heard me, Sir Huntley. I have made up my mind. There is nothing you could say that will change it. We won't speak of this again."

Jack and I never did speak of it again. And he never showed me the letter, just as I requested. I never again saw that look of pity on his face. I had seen that look all too often while I was grow-ing up. I was surrounded by faces filled with pity when I was a girl. I wouldn't have it in my new home.

I was starting a new life.

I spent my days happily in our large country estate, and every so often I would travel back to London to see Mama. Life was good with Jack. We threw lavish parties, inviting all the young bright things. And we often traveled to America, to see Jack's holdings there.

Jack and I did all the things I ever dreamed of growing up. We visited all the exotic places I fancied. All I had to do was make my wishes known, and Jack made all the arrangements. He was the best traveling companion. Always up for adventure. Always charming the locals. There was nothing he wouldn't try. From riding unruly camels when we went to Egypt to exploring the ruins of Angkor Wat . . . from lazily gliding in a gondola in Venice to living our best lives in a luxury apartment in Manhattan . . . the world was ours. It was the life I always imagined for myself. And when we made our way home, we had the grandest parties.

But nothing, I mean nothing, topped my twenty-fifth birthday party.

Of course Jack had thrown me the most extravagant party. It really was the biggest event of the season. I think the only party bigger was our wedding day. (I mean, how can you outdo a wedding at Westminster Abbey?)

Jack went all out. There were ice sculptures of me modeled after various important women of history, chocolate fountains, trays upon trays of caviar and toast points, bands in every wing of the house, and the ballroom was simply packed with the who's who of London society. Plus, there was a smattering of Hollywood thrown in for good measure, to keep things interesting. It was a night to remember. It was far from an intimate affair, so Mama decided she wouldn't attend. Instead, she sent me a marvelous gift: a fur coat, her signature gift.

I was living the grandest life I could wish for. I was married to the love of my life; my mother was safely tucked away in my childhood home; I was rich, beautiful, and happy. I was Lady Cruella De Vil.

But of course, isn't it always the case that the higher you fly, the farther you fall? And I would indeed fall, farther than I could have possibly imagined.

## CHAPTER XIII

# THE LITTLE
## BLACK DRESS

How shall I start this chapter? Should I tell you where I was when I heard the news? What I was wearing? How it changed my life in ways I thought could only be true in nightmares?

I was visiting my mother in London, the Monday after my birthday soiree. I wore a black slip dress, my jade earrings, and a white fur coat with red lining that Mama had given me for my twenty-fifth birthday. My shoes and gloves were red, and my handbag was made of white fur and dripping with white fox tails with black tips. As usual, I looked magnificent. "Simply stunning," Jack said, when I kissed him goodbye and left him to his work while I spent the afternoon with Mama.

"Now, don't be too long in London, my love, or I will miss you terribly," Jack said. He was sitting at his desk going over some paperwork.

"You have plenty to keep you occupied while I'm away, my darling," I said. He laughed, taking a sip of his drink and rattling the ice cubes that were left at the bottom of the glass.

"I will miss you nevertheless," he said.

"We just spent the most glorious evening together, my love." I kissed him on the cheek. "Thank you again for such a lovely evening. It was the best birthday I could ever wish for." He flashed his Clark Gable smile, the smile I now realize reminded me of my papa.

"Yes, but I had to share you with all of our guests. I want some time alone with you. Oh, wait." He snapped his fingers. "I haven't given you your gift." He took a little box out of his breast pocket.

"You already gave me the perfect gift, Jack. The party." He just smiled and opened the little box, revealing a beautiful jade ring. "Oh, my love! It matches my earrings." He put the ring on my finger.

"I know, Cruella. I had it made specially." He really was the most thoughtful husband.

"Blast," I said, looking at my watch. "Mama is expecting me." I kissed him quickly. "I really do love you so much, my Crackerjack. I'm so sorry, but I really do have to run." I had no idea it would be the last time I told him I loved him, or saw his handsome smile. But I am jumping ahead.

I went to London to see my mama so I could give her all the details about my birthday party, and it really was a lovely afternoon together. We sat in the morning room as we had so often while I was growing up, and it felt like old times.

"Oh, my darling girl, you look magnificent. Tell me you loved your party! Tell me you love the fur coat I got you! Oh, Cruella, tell me you love me, and you're not angry that I wanted to celebrate with you on my own rather than come to your party!" I was so pleased with Mama's transformation. She had been a completely different woman ever since I signed over my fortune. I guess it goes to show you that money really can buy happiness.

"Of course I'm not angry with you, Mama! I love you!" I said, laughing, as we air-kissed to keep our lipstick off each other's cheeks.

"Where is that wretched girl with the tea?" she asked, ringing the bell. "This place has gone to the dogs since you stole Jackson away from me!" She rang the bell again. Just then a scrawny, timid-looking maid came blundering into the room. I hadn't seen her before. She must have been a new addition to the staff.

"Yes, Lady De Vil?" she asked, her voice squeaking like a little mouse. She looked rather frightened of my mother. Or perhaps it was me she was afraid of. I was becoming quite a well-known socialite, after all. I wondered how my mother could deal with such a creature lurking around her house. She looked like the sort who peeked around corners before entering the room.

"Good grief! My mother has been ringing for tea for what seems like an eternity and you dare come in empty-handed. My servants wouldn't dream of such slipshod service!" I said, thoroughly frustrated she hadn't yet brought in the tea.

"Shall I bring the tea then, Lady De Vil?" she asked, clearly afraid to make eye contact with me.

"Forget the tea, Sarah. Have Mrs. Web bring me that bottle I had her get from the cellar. My daughter and I are celebrating."

"Yes, my lady," she said, skittering away. I rolled my eyes.

"Really, Mama. This is intolerable. The Spider really should take care to hire better maids. That girl looks like she had just jumped out of her own skin. And do we really have to have *her* bring the champagne into the morning room? You know how much I detest the the Spider."

"Oh, Cruella, please don't ruin our time with your incessant need to call people by silly nicknames. You'd think you would have outgrown it by now. We're here to celebrate. I want to hear all about your birthday," she said, looking at the clock.

"Mama, why are you watching the clock? Are

we expecting someone?" I wondered where the hell Mrs. Web was with our celebratory drinks. "Really, Mama. How long does it take to grab a bottle and a couple of glasses? And why on earth didn't they ever send up the tea in the first place? It's well past teatime! What is Mrs. Baddeley doing down there, anyway? How long does it take to boil water and cut the crusts off little sandwiches?"

"Mrs. Baddeley left us some time ago, Cruella," Mama said, as if I somehow should have known. "She decided she wanted to work for a smaller household." I was shocked. I couldn't imagine Belgrave Place without her.

"Really? You didn't tell me. Where exactly did she go?"

"Oh, I don't know, Cruella. Some young couple of no consequence. She said it was a cozy little place, near a park. Though it's been my experience when someone calls something cozy what they really mean is a hovel. I can dig up the exact address if it means that much to you," she said, looking at the clock again.

"Mama! Why are you looking at the clock again? Who are we expecting? And where are the bloody drinks?"

"Cruella! Language!" my mother scolded. It was all too funny being back at home. Mama was scolding me like old times—me, a married woman with a house of my own! But that was our dynamic these days. I enjoyed scandalizing her, and she enjoyed calling me out on it. And I don't think I ever really shocked her. I think she just enjoyed acting as though I had. Or at least that is what I always told myself. It was just our way.

Just then the Spider came into the room—without the bottle, I noticed. "Lady De Vil," she said. Both of us answered, "Yes?" Only a little thrown off, the Spider continued.

"Sir Huntley is here. I showed him into the sitting room."

"Please show him in here in a few moments, Mrs. Web. And for heaven's sake, please do bring in that bottle."

"Yes, Mrs. Web, why don't you go get it before

you ask in Sir Huntley," I said, dismissing her.

"Now, Cruella, I won't have you dismissing the servants in my own home. I know you don't care for Mrs. Web, but I do have to live with her." I laughed.

"And I'm very sorry that you do. But why have you invited Sir Huntley? I thought we were spending the afternoon together, to celebrate my birthday."

"And so we are, my dear. Your twenty-fifth birthday. Your father's money, your inheritance, is officially yours today, my dearest. I thought you would be eager to make the transfer to my accounts official, as we discussed." It had completely slipped my mind. Of course I had intended to transfer over the money, but I hadn't expected to do it that afternoon.

"Yes, of course," I said, smiling. Though of course it had taken me by surprise, I really was quite happy to do this for my mama. It made me feel proud that I could provide for her in this way. To do something for her after all of her years of devotion to me.

Sir Huntley stood in the morning room doorway and cleared his throat. "Good afternoon, ladies. Mrs. Web said I was to come in." He was such a timid man. Like a little blind mole who only came out of his burrow to make his clients sign documents. A mole in a tweed suit.

"Yes, please, Sir Huntley, do sit down," I said, making my mother flinch. I had done it again. I was directing people around in her home. Well, perhaps I was taking possession of the house by directing my mother's servants about one last time before I gave the house and my money over to her. I didn't see that then, of course, but now when I think back on it, I am almost sure that is what I was doing.

"I don't have time to stay, ladies. I'm just bringing by the paperwork you requested." Sir Huntley shot a nervous glance at my mama. You'd think this was a house of horrors the way everyone tiptoed around us.

"I wonder why you didn't just have it delivered then?" I asked, trying not to laugh at the poor man.

He was shaking so intensely I thought he was going to drop his briefcase.

"I wanted to be sure this was still your wish, Lady Cruella," he said, this time keeping his hands from shaking by grasping his briefcase so tightly I could see his knuckles turning white. "It's been several years since we first discussed this."

"Are you quite all right, Sir Huntley?" I eyed his shaking hands. "Could I perhaps offer you some tea? I'm sure my mama's maid would be happy to tiptoe down to the kitchen and retrieve some, though it might take an hour or two." I laughed at my joke, but my mother just glowered at me.

"No, thank you, my lady." He had a concerned look on his face, and suddenly I felt bad for taking delight in his nervousness. He was just looking out for my interest, just as my sweet papa had asked him. So I reassured him the best I knew how.

"It is indeed my greatest wish, I assure you." I tried to put him at ease with a smile.

Sir Huntley, with slightly steadier hands, opened his briefcase. He took out the papers, inspected them for a moment, and then placed them on a round table to the left of the love seat that faced the fireplace.

"Well then, if both ladies will just sign, I will be on my way," he said, and then added quickly, "That is, if Lady Cruella is absolutely sure."

"I am sure, Sir Huntley," I said, quite firmly this time. Did he think I was so fickle in my decisions? I could slap the man for asking the question in front of Mama. "Shall we sign, Mama?" I asked. Sir Huntley provided a fountain pen, though at first the blasted thing didn't work! I had to shake it several times, until finally it sprayed spots of black ink all over him. I stifled a laugh, signing my name on the dotted line. Mama added her signature below mine. And the deed was done. I had given Mama my fortune. And I was happy to do it.

"Very well," he said. He looked defeated. His jowls seemed to hang lower than usual, and his eyes looked heavily hooded as he gathered up the papers and put them back into his briefcase. Then he paused and looked up at me. "Lady Cruella, if you ever need anything, anything at all, please give me a ring." And like a wounded dog he left quite quickly, before Mama could even ring to have someone show him out.

"Well, that was theatrical!" I said, laughing. Mrs. Web came into the room then. Empty-handed, wouldn't you know it. "Good lord, woman, where is the champagne?" The Spider just stood there quiet and still, looking as if she had seen a ghost. Or perhaps her own reflection. I turned to my mother. "This is outrageous, Mama. What is going on with your staff? Is everyone hell-bent on driving me mad today?"

"Cruella, what is wrong with you? Do calm down." My mother put a hand to her forehead, as if I was giving her a headache. "And what are you doing? Stop fidgeting with your earring! Those are the earrings your father gave you, think how upset you'd be if you lost one."

"They're bothering me for some reason," I said, twisting the jade ball again, hoping it would make a difference.

"Well, take them off. They're making you irritable." We had completely forgotten about Mrs. Web. She stood there staring at us, looking ghastly, like someone had drained all the blood from her face. "What's the matter, Mrs. Web? Why have you still not brought in our drinks?" My mother was beginning to sound testy as well. Perhaps I was rubbing off on her.

Mrs. Web just stood there staring for a moment before she finally spoke.

"Lady Cruella, it's your husband."

"What about my husband?" I asked, still distracted by my earring and wondering what she could possibly be going on about. "Is he here?"

"I don't know how to say this, Lady Cruella, but he's been killed."

"That's impossible," I scoffed. "Jack would never allow himself to be killed! There must be some mistake." The Spider may have been ghastly, but this seemed like a very cruel trick to play on me, even for her.

"I'm so sorry, my lady, but it's true. Jackson and

the rest of your staff are downstairs. They're very shaken up." It didn't make any sense. Everything felt confusing and surreal. "Why are they here? Where's Jackson? Send him up so I can speak with him," I said.

"I think he's in shock, my lady," she said, looking at me with pity in her eyes. I couldn't stand it. Everyone was always looking at me like that, for my whole life, and I had had enough. I couldn't abide it from *her* of all people. I just stood there.

"I think my daughter is also in shock, Mrs. Web," my mother said. Her voice was surprisingly gentle. "Please send Jackson up here at once so we can speak to him." Mrs. Web just stood there for another moment, unsure, unmoving.

"Send him up here at once!" I screamed. "Send him up this moment! Do you understand? Go!" The woman went scuttling out of the room, and I was left with my mama. Alone. Was I alone now? Was my Crackerjack really gone? I couldn't fathom it. I didn't believe it. There was no way my Jack was dead. Not Crackerjack. He was too strong to die. Too stubborn to allow himself to be killed. It didn't make sense. There had to be some sort of mistake.

Miss Pricket came into the morning room instead of Jackson. She looked dreadful. Her face, hands, and clothing were smudged with some sort of soot, and her hair was mussed. I felt so relieved to see her that I almost started to cry.

"Miss Pricket! What's happened? Where's Jackson?" I said.

"Oh, my lady, I am so sorry," was all she could say before she started crying so hard she was shaking with every breath.

"What happened? Please, tell me what happened. No one can seem to tell me what's happened to my husband!"

Miss Pricket looked at Mama nervously. Her hands were shaking.

"Have some brandy, girl, and sit down and tell my daughter what's happened. This is madness. Where is Jackson?" My mother was raising her voice, clearly as frustrated as I was. Miss Pricket poured herself a little glass of brandy and drank it down all at once, then composed herself.

"Mr. Jackson is downstairs with the others. Mrs. Web called for the doctor when we arrived. The doctor is looking at Mr. Jackson now, that's why I came up." And she started to cry again. Sobbing uncontrollably, she told the story between great heaving breaths. "Oh, Lady Cruella, I am so sorry. We did everything we could, but the fire was too great. Jackson tried to save him. He wanted to. But the fire was out of control—we couldn't even get to the study. Our way was blocked, and it was spreading throughout the house. Only those who were downstairs made it out of the house, Lady Cruella. When the fire brigade finally arrived, there was nothing of the house left." I couldn't believe it. Jack *must* have made his way out.

"Are you sure Jack was in his study? Maybe he went out?" I asked, desperate.

"No, my lady. He was in his study all afternoon. Jackson would have known if he went out," she said, shaking with tears.

261

"Did the fire brigade find his body?" I asked, convinced he had slipped out without anyone noticing.

"They haven't, my lady. But they are still investigating, trying to find the source of the fire."

"Then there is a chance he wasn't killed," I said. "Jack can't be dead. He can't! I won't believe it until I see it for myself. Have someone bring a car around."

"But my lady, there is nothing to see but ashes and ruin. There is nothing left."

✤ ✤ ✤ ✤

Miss Pricket was right. There was nothing left. The house, all of our belongings. Everything was gone. Jack was gone.

I never forgave Jackson and the others for surviving the fire. I didn't understand why someone couldn't save him. None of the servants could tell me what happened. Not coherently, anyway. The only people who made it out of the house unhurt were the staff downstairs. Everyone in the main part of the house was killed. The fire marshal said there was likely some sort of mishap with the fireplace in the study. He said there was an enormous amount of rubbish, papers, and files stuffed into the fireplace, and that he found Jack's body sitting near the fireplace in what was left of his chair. He thought Jack had fallen asleep sitting there and that's why he hadn't realized the room caught fire. That the smoke had caused him to become unconscious and that's why he didn't wake.

"Then he didn't feel pain, he didn't suffer in the flames?" I asked.

"No, my lady. I don't think so. There is no sign that he was trying to get out of the room. In cases like this we would see evidence that the person tried to break a window, or make it to a doorway. Your husband was still sitting in his chair." Then he asked me the unthinkable. "Was your husband upset about anything, my lady? Had he shared any concerns he may be having?" I didn't understand. "I'm sorry my lady, but I have to ask. The papers, the debris in the fireplace. There was so much of it. It did look as if he was trying to burn those things on purpose."

"Don't be ridiculous. My husband was the happiest person I know. He wouldn't do something foolish. And he wasn't trying to hide some sort of shady skullduggery! I'm not entirely convinced that is his body you found! He wouldn't do that to me. He wouldn't leave me. He wouldn't."

We had no means of identifying Jack's body, or any of the servants' bodies that were found in the main house. For all I knew it was one of the footmen who died in Jack's study, sneaking a drink and a nap by the fire. Nothing of the body's clothes were left. Nothing of him. I became more convinced that Jack wasn't home when the fire broke out, so I waited. I waited in the ashes for my love to come home. I refused to leave, sure my Jack would come home to me. Mama finally sent a car for me and had me brought back to Belgrave Place. She had me take my old room, and instructed Jackson and the other survivors of the fire to stay downstairs, out of sight.

I locked myself up in my room for weeks, refusing to eat, refusing to believe my Jack was gone.

I still feel in my heart he is alive.

*The Little Black Dress*

I stayed locked in my old room at my mother's for about three weeks before she tried to force me out. But that is another chapter. Another part of the story. I don't wish to write about that now. It breaks my heart too much. I'd rather keep writing about my Jack. But what else is there to say? He's either dead or pretending to be dead. At one point I thought maybe he had left for some business trip without telling me. Perhaps some sort of emergency? I didn't know. I was grasping at any explanation I could think of. But it's been quite some time now since the fire. Everyone keeps telling me I should accept that the person in Jack's crypt is really Jack. My beloved Jack. My Crackerjack.

They tell me I should say goodbye, but I can't bring myself to say it. Not yet.

## CHAPTER XIV

# CRUELLA DE VIL

It had been almost a month since the fire. I was still staying with my mama in Belgrave Square, sequestered in my old room, refusing to see anyone. That is until the morning my mama came crashing into my room with a battalion of maids. She directed them like a great general, pointing them in various directions and barking orders.

"Rose! Open those curtains! It's depressing in here. And open a window. Lady Cruella hasn't had fresh air or sunlight in weeks!"

"Do not open those curtains!" I said from under the blankets, frightening my mother's maid. I wasn't about to get up. I didn't care how many maids my mother brought into my room. I was staying put. I pulled the duvet over my head and tried to hide from the mayhem that overtook my solitude.

From under my duvet I could see the room was filled with bright afternoon light, and I could make out the shadows of many servants scurrying around the room doing my mama's bidding.

"Violet, draw Lady Cruella a bath!" barked my mother, startling me. I had refused any visitors for weeks, and I wasn't used to all that noise and commotion. It was unsettling to be besieged by so much happening at once, and all I wanted to do was go back to sleep. I was exhausted and heartbroken. I didn't understand why my mama was trying to force me up.

"I'm not taking a bath!" I said from under the covers.

"Cruella, stop acting like a child and come out from under those covers at once! You will get out of that bed, bathe, and dress yourself!" my mother said. I could see her shadow standing over me from under the duvet.

"Sarah! Where's that tray I asked to be prepared for Lady Cruella?"

"In the hall, your ladyship," the maid said, rushing to go get it.

"I'm not hungry!" I yelled after her, but she was back with the tray before I could finish protesting. I could see her shadow standing over me, holding the tray and waiting for me to sit up.

"Cruella, sit up, and at least have a little something to eat." This time my mother's voice was raised. She was getting angry. And that was the last thing I wanted, so I reluctantly came out from under the covers, squinting because the room was flooded with light.

The room went silent. Everyone stared at me.

"My goodness! Everyone out of the room at once! Violet, call the doctor! Now!" My mama looked positively gobsmacked. All the maids scattered like frightened mice.

"What is it, Mama? What's wrong?" I asked. Her face was filled with a mixture of worry and horror. "Mama? What is it?"

"Nothing, my dear. Nothing," she said, petting my hand and trying to pretend everything was all right.

"Mama! What's the matter?" I said, getting up from the bed. She was starting to frighten me. "Tell me what's wrong, please!"

"It's your hair, Cruella. It's turned white!"

My mama has always been rather dramatic and prone to exaggeration. The fact was, only half of my hair had turned white. The other half was still pitch-black, as it had always been. But leave it to Mama to send the household into a panic over something as trivial as my hair color.

⚜ ⚜ ⚜ ⚜

Later that afternoon the doctor came by. My mother was fretting, coddling, and hovering so much he tried to send her out of the room.

"I have no intention of leaving the room, Dr. Humphrey. Just look at the state of her! Look at her hair. What in blazes caused that?"

"Lady De Vil has experienced a tremendous and sudden loss. She is suffering from shock and grief," he said.

"But will her hair go back to normal?" my mother asked. The doctor, however, didn't seem concerned for my hair.

"What worries me is how thin your daughter has become," he said, studying me. "I think with a little rest, more sunlight, and a sensible diet she will be blooming again."

After the doctor left, Mama talked me into taking dinner in the dining room that evening. She instructed the maid to lay out a lovely dress for me to wear to dinner while I was in the bath, but I couldn't bring myself to wear anything other than my black dress. The one I was wearing when I learned my Jack had died. I found it cleaned and hanging in the closet next to a number of dresses and nightgowns my mama had purchased for me and had sent up to my room. It still looked good on me. Slinky, black, and stunning. It went perfectly with my jade earrings and the new jade ring Jack had given me for my birthday.

As I stood in my old room looking at myself in the mirror, I seemed a new person: thinner, older, somehow wiser and more elegant. I had changed. And I was living in an entirely different world. One without my Jack. It seemed fitting that I, too, was different. I decided I liked my new beauty. I liked the severity of it. I even liked my hair. Only one thing was missing: my fur coat. I put it on. I was myself again. I went downstairs. I was ready.

## CHAPTER XV

# GOODBYE, BELGRAVIA

That was to be my last evening with my mama, though I didn't know it at the time. The table was set beautifully, and my mother's cook had outdone herself, preparing all my favorite dishes in an effort to tempt me. I sat across from my mother, picking at my plate. She looked at me nervously, as she had been doing since she'd seen my transformation.

"Cruella, I've arranged for all your favorites. Won't you eat something?" she asked.

"Thank Mrs. Baddeley for me, please," I said. "And give her my apologies for not having an appetite." My mother looked at me as if I was losing my mind.

"Mrs. Baddeley has left our household, Cruella. I told you, remember?" The fact was, I had forgotten.

"How am I to be expected to remember these insignificant, mundane household changes, Mother?" I asked dismissively, but the truth was I wondered how I had managed to forget.

"You're right, my dear," she said, still looking at me with concern. I assumed she was still getting used to my hair. Then, "Cruella, why are you wearing the fur coat I gave you for your birthday at the dinner table?"

"You didn't get me this coat, Mama. Jack did. It was a gift for my birthday," I said, smiling at her. She looked so confused.

"My darling, *I* got you that coat for your birthday." She looked at me with narrowed eyes. It now occurs to me that I must have been suffering from some sort of memory loss due to the shock of losing Jack. It's no wonder my poor mama was so concerned. But then I remembered.

"So you did, Mama. I remember now. You gave

me the coat, Jack gave me the ring, and Papa gave me my earrings."

"Yes, my dear," she said, looking no less worried.

"I don't know what I would do without you, Mama. I can't imagine being on my own right now. I'm so lucky to have such a sweet mama, so willing to take care of me."

And I was so happy to be in my childhood home, to be surrounded by things that made me feel comforted.

"You really must eat, Cruella. You've become so thin," she said, clearly still worried.

"I don't wish to eat, Mama. Please don't worry. I think I may be suffering from a lapse of memory," I said, trying to make her feel better.

"The doctor said that may happen. Perhaps I better have Mrs. Web call the doctor and tell him."

"Don't fret, Mama," I said. "I assure you I am quite well."

"Did Violet not lay out that new dress I bought you, Cruella? That dress you're wearing is hanging off you."

"Violet? Oh yes, the maid. Yes, she did, Mama, but I wanted to wear this one," I said, giving her a sly look.

"Well, it's morbid, wearing the same dress . . ." But she stopped herself. She was clearly getting rather vexed with me, but tempering her anger because she was worried about my health.

"I'm sorry, Mama." I pushed my plate away, deciding I was tired of pretending I was going to eat dinner. "I really don't wish to eat dinner, Mama."

"I know you're distraught, dear. Let's move into the drawing room. I have something important I want to discuss with you."

I rolled my eyes. "Why can't we just sit in here? And what is it we need to discuss?" I asked.

"Well, for starters, we really must do something about your staff. I can't keep them on here in addition to my own. Won't you change your mind about keeping them on yourself? You will, of course, be needing a staff you can trust once you're in your new home."

"My new home?" I asked, blinking. I had no idea what she was talking about. What new home? I intended on staying right where I was. In the place I felt safest. In the home my father left me.

"Of course, my dear, you'll be wanting to start your new life in a new home of your own. Or maybe you will want to travel? Whatever you decide, my dear."

"Well, Mama, I was thinking of asking if I could stay here. We can make some sort of arrangements for Jackson and Miss Pricket."

My mother looked very uncomfortable.

"Well, the fact is, Cruella, I am closing up the house."

"What do you mean, closing up the house?" I didn't understand. I just gave her the house and now she was closing it?

"I mean exactly that." She poured us both some tea, deciding she couldn't wait to have Mrs. Web show us into the drawing room.

"But I thought I would stay here. At least for a while longer," I said. "If you want to travel, I can stay here and take care of the house. I promise I won't be mean to Mrs. Web."

"That won't be possible, Cruella. I've arranged to have everything crated and sold at auction. I have two weeks before I have to vacate for the new owners, after which I don't plan to return to London for quite some time. I'm letting all of the staff go except for Mrs. Web. She is coming along with me as my companion."

"Two weeks? So you're not closing up the house, Mama. You've sold it. Right out from under me."

"It's my house, Cruella. I can do with it as I please." I was livid. I had just lost my own home and my husband. All I wanted was to stay someplace where I felt safe. I couldn't believe she'd sold the house so quickly, and without telling me about it. Sir Huntley had warned me this might happen.

"The moment I signed everything over to you, you've sold it. I can't believe I was so foolish."

I stood up, unable to sit still. I was so angry with her. But there was nothing to be done about it now. There was no sense in fighting about it with my mother at that point. Anyway, she changed the subject and saved me from having to pursue the conversation.

"Speaking of Sir Huntley, I've taken the liberty of inviting him over after dinner this evening. I did extend an invitation to dinner as well, but he declined, saying he would come after the dinner hour. He's eager to speak with you about Jack's will."

It seemed my mother was full of surprises that evening.

"I'm not ready to discuss Jack's will, Mama. I really wish you had asked me if I was up to seeing my solicitor," I said, slamming down the glass.

"Sir Huntley is more than our solicitor, Cruella. He's been with our family for a long time. He's almost one of the family."

I suddenly burst out laughing. I was in disbelief. Who was this woman? Surely not my mama. "Sir Huntley! A member of the family? Come on now, you despise the man!" I said. "What exactly are you playing at, Mama? I may have suffered a lapse of memory, but I do remember your utter contempt for Sir Huntley."

"Very well, Cruella. I hardly know what to say to you while you're in this state. You're acting so strangely. I'm just trying to make things easier between us. . . ."

But before she could say anything more, Jackson came into the room.

"Are the ladies ready to go into the drawing room? Sir Huntley will be arriving shortly," he said, giving me a sad look. Part of me wanted to stand up and hug the man. I felt like a lost little girl, sitting in my mother's dining room. And I felt so alone. Papa and Anita were gone, and now Jack. And Mama was abandoning me. Who else did I have left but Jackson and Miss Pricket? But I couldn't forgive him for not saving Jack. And I couldn't stand the pity.

"Are *the ladies* ready to go into the drawing room?" I sneered. "Seeing as we're *all ladies here*, with the exception of you, Jackson, I would say that *the ladies* are indeed ready to go to the sitting room."

"Cruella, what is wrong with you?" My mother looked horrified.

"Why do you suppose it's just we ladies dining this evening? Why do you suppose my husband isn't here with us?" I knew I was breaking Jackson's heart, but I didn't care.

"Cruella, stop this at once. Jackson, I'm so sorry." My mother was mortified. And part of me was appalled by my own behavior, but I couldn't stop myself. I was heartbroken, but also annoyed. My earring was bothering me again, and the more it irritated me, the more I wanted to scream. So I took it out on poor Jackson.

It was as if an overwhelming rage was exploding within me, and I was directing it at this poor man, a man who had treated me like his own daughter when I was growing up. But I couldn't stop myself. I couldn't forgive him. I couldn't stop hating him. Even if now was the time I needed him most.

"I told you to keep him out of my sight, Mama!" I said, throwing the glass across the room.

And poor Jackson left without a word. And the

room was suddenly silent, just for a moment. All I was left with was my rage. "How dare you parade him in here like that! I told you I didn't wish to see him!"

"How dare *I*? How dare *you* speak to Jackson that way! Control yourself, Cruella! What has come over you? You've hurt Jackson's feelings. He's always doted on you since you were a little girl, and I am sure he feels terrible about what happened to your Jack! It's not Jackson's fault he survived the fire and Jack did not!" she said. And she was right. But I couldn't make myself see it in that moment. My hate was too strong. Everything was crumbling around me. I was falling down a deep hole with nothing to cling to.

"Hurt Jackson's feelings indeed! Since when have you given one jot about our staff's feelings, Mother?" I snapped, fidgeting with my earring, twisting it and trying to make it stop pinching.

"Cruella, please calm down, and do stop fiddling with your damned earring. Sir Huntley will be here soon if he's not already in the drawing room, so please lower your voice and compose yourself."

"That's rich, Mother. You telling me to compose myself for Sir Huntley." I laughed so hard I almost choked. "I'm sure you have much to do to prepare for your move. I can talk to Sir Huntley on my own."

I walked out of the dining room, feeling a bit unsteady on my feet. Everything was changing. My Jack was gone, and soon my childhood home would be gone. Where would I go? Well, at least I had money enough to do whatever I liked. Live wherever I wanted. I could hardly imagine living in one of Jack's houses without him. What I really wanted was to stay in my old home, but that wasn't an option. I thought of buying it from the new owners. I would ask my mother who they were and offer them an absurd amount to take it off their hands. No matter the cost, it would be worth it. I wanted to return to my original life plan. I wanted to live alone in my father's house. And maybe I would keep on Jackson and Miss Pricket. They were, after all, the only people I had left. I could learn to forgive them, in time. And maybe, just maybe, I would see if Anita would be up for an adventure. Surely a life with me would be far better than settling for a life with that foolish musician.

Then I remembered. Sir Huntley was waiting for me.

## CHAPTER XVI

# GOODBYE, MAMA

After Sir Huntley left, Mama came into the room to check on me. I was sitting on the leather love seat. I was numb. I had nothing. Nothing but the deed to a house I didn't even want. But I will get to that.

"My dear. Are you quite all right? Sir Huntley looked dreadful as he left. Did he have bad news?"

I couldn't bring myself to tell her I had been reduced to almost nothing. I couldn't disappoint her like that.

"No, Mama. I'm just sad," I said. "And I'm sorry for how I acted. How I spoke to you earlier. I don't know what came over me. I haven't been myself." I twisted the jade ring Jack had given me. She sat down next to me on the love seat, wrapping her arms around me.

"Well, it's no wonder, my darling. I felt the same way after your father died. That's why I left, my dear Cruella. I was so angry. I felt so abandoned and so alone."

*She wouldn't have been alone if she had stayed home with me,* I thought, but I didn't say so. I had lost everyone I loved. I didn't want to lose my mother as well, even if I was confused and angered by her choices.

"I was afraid of taking my anger out on you after your father died, my Cruella," she said. "But I thought of you every day I was gone."

I smiled at her. "And you sent me gifts. I knew you were thinking of me. I knew you loved me, Mama." My heart softened to her. I felt like I understood her better now that I was suffering the same way she had.

"But we are both in the same boat now, aren't we, dear? Both abandoned. Both untethered. Both able to distinguish ourselves anyway we see it. Cruella, use that great fortune of yours and make the best possible life for yourself. You never intended to marry anyway. Travel the world. Build yourself a beautiful life."

I broke down crying. I had no means to do any of it. And I hated telling Mama.

"I have nothing, Mama. Nothing at all except what you see here. Everything is gone," I said, crying into my mother's arms.

"Oh, my dear, I know you loved Jack very much, and it might feel that way, especially at first, but it isn't so. You still have his fortune. Just as I have your father's." She released me from her embrace and took both of my hands. "I promise you, Cruella, everything will be okay."

"But it won't, Mama. Jack left me nothing— there was nothing to leave me. His businesses were underwater, and what was left was seized by his unscrupulous business partners. He was struggling the whole time we were married, and I knew none of it. I have nothing left."

"This is shocking! How could Jack let something like that happen?" she asked.

"Sir Huntley thinks he may have been struggling for a long time, losing money steadily to his partners. Of course he didn't tell me a thing about it. You know Jack, always putting on a happy facade. Always wanting to make me happy."

Mama was in shock. "But what of his family money? Surely they couldn't seize that?" she said.

"I . . . I signed something," I stammered. "Before the wedding. A prenuptial agreement. I didn't think anything of it at the time. I thought Jack and I would be together forever. But now he's gone and his family's money is protected from even me."

"This is scandalous, Cruella! Where will you go? What will you do to support yourself? I don't understand how this could have happened?" She was hysterical and it wasn't helping.

"I think it's my fault, Mama. Maybe if I hadn't hidden away after Jack died I could have fought it all, but Sir Huntley said there was nothing I could have done."

"Well, Cruella, then he is right. If he says there was nothing you could have done then there is no sense in thinking otherwise. I would just like to know how you're expected to live? I can't believe Jack would leave you penniless!" She stood abruptly from the love seat and walked over to the fireplace.

"Well, it seems Papa left me De Vil Hall in the event something like this should happen. Something like insurance in the event of disaster."

"Well then, you're taken care of. Brilliant. I don't have to worry about you." She looked lovingly at a photo of my papa on the mantel.

"Mama, the income from the tenants and farmers is barely enough for the upkeep on the house and lands, let alone enough to live on. I thought perhaps I could travel with you. Or you would reconsider and let me live here. Is it too late to say you want to keep the house?"

"Listen, my dear, I think the country air will do you some good. Some time away from the city. You have to reclaim yourself, Cruella. Create a new life. Just as I did when your father died."

"But how? How will I do that?"

"Cruella, you're a strong, resourceful young

woman. You're just like me. Your father always said so, anyway. Look at me. I lost my husband and my fortune, and now I have it back! You can do the same! Distinguish yourself, my girl. And what better way to do it than with a completely clean slate? And in a new home, De Vil Hall. Oh, that will be so lovely for you, my Cruella."

I had vague memories of De Vil Hall from when I was younger. We didn't spend much time there because it was too rustic for Mama. Surrounded by a little village, with farms. Nothing but rolling hills as far as the eye could see. It was hours and hours out of London. So far from my friends, and the life I had built for myself with Jack.

I felt as if I was being exiled, hidden away so my mother wouldn't be embarrassed by her penniless daughter. Hidden away because I had been withered and aged by my grief. What better place to send me than the old De Vil estate in the country? A place that would later be known as Hell Hall.

## CHAPTER XVII

# HELL HALL

Even though De Vil Hall was grander than I remembered, it was a lonely place. It was a place out of another time, with its velvet couches, ornate wooden furniture, and gold-framed oil paintings of my father's long-dead relatives peering at me. It was a dead place. A place to die. And that's what I intended to do. I spent my days and nights missing my Jack, missing my parents, and missing my old life. I languished there, too heartbroken to eat. Too heartbroken to do anything other than cry. I cried and screamed into the night so often that De Vil Hall became known as Hell Hall in the neighboring village. I decided to embrace it.

# Hell Hall

I couldn't find my way out of the darkness or see a light at the end of my wretched misery. I cried until I was too exhausted to cry anymore. I'd fall asleep and dream of the days when I had been truly happy, walking in the woods on Miss Upturn's grounds with Anita—only to wake up in this dark place with its peeling wallpaper and groaning floors. I was so angry with my mother for abandoning me to this. I grew angry with Jack for not providing for me after his death. I was upset with myself for not listening to my father's warnings about my mother, and angry with him for not doing enough to protect me from her. I was alone. And it was all my fault. I had pushed Anita away. I'd never believed her warnings. But she had been right all along. Everyone had.

I gave Mama everything that should have been mine, and she turned her back on me, leaving me to the howling winds and barking dogs of the countryside.

I kept replaying my last conversation with my mother. Wondering why I didn't rail on her when she didn't offer to help me. I had always been afraid to make her angry. Afraid if I spoke out she would abandon me. In the end, none of it mattered. That's exactly what she had done anyway.

I can't say how much time passed. How long I spent lamenting my old life. How many lonely nights I cried into the darkness with no one to hear me or comfort me. I wasn't myself. I had tossed aside the things that reminded me of those who abandoned me. I stopped wearing my furs and my jade earrings—I even stopped wearing the jade ring Jack had given me. Seeing them brought only anger and more tears. I started to see how my life had come to ruins. How I was brought to this. I thought I saw it all so clearly, the way I had that Christmas when Anita and I were still close. Everyone in the kitchen that night had been my real family, and I had done nothing but push them away. I missed Anita and Perdita. If only I could have afforded to keep them on, I would have brought them with me.

In my desperation and loneliness I decided to call Anita. I had been in bed for days. Exhausted, weak, and alone. But I picked up the phone and called one of the few people I felt had ever truly loved me. She was surprised to hear from me. We had been writing occasionally, of course, but hadn't spoken until that night.

"Hello, Anita darling. It's me, Cruella."

"Cruella? Hello. How are you?"

"I'm not well, Anita. I was wondering if you would agree to meet with me. There are so many things I would like to say to you. So many things I am sorry for, but I'd rather talk with you in person. And I would so love to see Perdita."

"Oh, Cruella. I'm not sure if that is a good idea. Things went so wrong between us. I'm just not sure."

"Anita, please. She is mine, after all. A gift from my father. Would you deny me just one little visit, and the opportunity to tell you how truly sorry I am for . . . well, everything?" There was a pause on the other end of the line, and a small sigh.

"Of course not, Cruella. Let's meet at the Park Café. Do you know where it is?"

"I do. And you will bring Perdita along?"

"Yes, Cruella. She will be with me."

"Thank you, Anita. You have no idea how much this means to me."

"You're welcome. And Cruella . . ." She paused. "I'm happy you called. I have missed you."

"Oh, Anita. I have missed you, too." And then I hung up before she could hear me trying to choke back the tears. I hadn't expected her to say that she missed me.

I was so anxious to see her that I stayed up almost all night pacing those lonely halls. I couldn't sleep. I couldn't eat. I could do nothing but regret the choices I had made. Anita was right. My father was right. And I was drowning in my bad choices. But all would be well when I saw Anita. All would be as it was before. I would have my life back. I would have my friend back.

## CHAPTER XVIII

# ᛈPERDITA

ᛁ was so nervous that morning while getting ready to meet Anita. I had gotten myself into a tizzy trying to find the right outfit. I wanted everything to be perfect. I tried on everything in my closet, first putting it on, then flinging it on the bed or the floor, until I finally arrived at my black dress.

*The* black dress. You know the one. The only dress that felt right. The only dress that looked right. I had so wanted to leave my old trappings behind, to leave the old Cruella behind, but I couldn't bring myself to leave the house without them. Quite at the last moment I decided to wear the ring Jack had had made for me, and the earrings given to me by my sweet papa. Wearing my most cherished pieces made me feel as if I was becoming myself again. Something within me shifted—especially when I put on my earrings. I felt a tingling sensation. A feeling that intensified as I made my way back to London.

The one thing I left behind was my fur coat. I couldn't stand to see the thing. It reminded me of my mama, and I was worried it would remind Anita of my mama as well.

After a long drive I finally arrived in London and found the little café, exactly where Anita said it would be. Not that I doubted her. I was feeling so much better being back in London. I could breathe. And I felt more confident. I was filled with a vitality I hadn't felt in a long time, and I was happy I'd made the trip. There was something about wearing that dress and my jewelry again that gave me courage. Or perhaps it was being back in London, or the prospect of seeing Anita again, or kissing Perdita's soft black nose. I wasn't quite sure. Whatever it was,

I was happy to be there. And to be feeling like my old self again.

I parked nearby, around the corner, and made my way to the café on foot. As I rounded the corner, I saw them before they saw me. Perdita was with her, as promised. Anita was in a pretty little sundress, reading her book in the sunshine, sipping away at her coffee, and Perdita was curled up at her feet. She had turned into a beautiful dog with a long, pointed snout and delicate features. She wore a slender blue collar with a gold tag. Anita had been taking good care of her. But I'd never doubted she would. Not for a moment. I stood there for the longest time, just watching them. Envying them their happiness. Just sitting there in the sun. Anita not even looking up from her book or at her watch, curious where I might be. She was carefree and happy. I felt like a monster in comparison. Too tall, too thin, too sad, and too angry to even belong in the same world as them.

I had missed so much time with them both, and there was so much I wanted to say to Anita. So many things to apologize for. Or at least I thought so at the time.

As I approached their table, Perdita opened her eyes, and for a moment I thought she knew me. "Cruella!" Anita stood up to greet me, stepping in front of Perdita and preventing me from reaching down to say hello.

"Hello, Anita," I said.

Anita looked down at Perdita and tried to coax her to come out from behind her to say hello. "Perdita. You remember Cruella. Say hello." She slowly moved her head around the right side of Anita's legs, peering out at me, but wouldn't come over to greet me. I have to admit I was crushed. I had pinned all my hopes on this meeting with them. "I'm sorry, Cruella. She isn't usually like this. I'm sure once she gets to know you better she will warm up to you." Sweet Anita. Always trying to save my feelings. But I thought maybe she was right. Maybe Perdita would remember me.

"Oh, Perdita. It hurts me that you don't remember me. You know, you were once mine," I said. Of course the dog didn't know what I was saying. But maybe it was more for Anita's benefit anyway.

"Oh, Cruella. Please don't take it that way," she said, looking sincerely sad for me. It was that same look they all gave me. I hated that look.

I had been ready to tell Anita everything, my entire story. To tell her she was right about my mama, right about how I had treated my servants, and how very sorry I was for being angry at her for pursuing her own dreams. But something happened as I sat there. I honestly can't tell you exactly what it was, but something shifted within me. Something sparked. It felt like a current washing over me, a much more intense version of the feeling I'd had when I put on my old trappings, a feeling that grew the closer I got to London. Now, I'm not saying London had some magical effect on me. I don't believe in such things. But something did happen. I felt an inkling of my transformation the moment I got ready to leave Hell Hall, and it just got stronger and stronger as I made my way to London. I have a theory, but you will probably think I'm mad. I'll let you make of it what you will. Whatever happened, however it came to be, I am thankful.

As Anita told me about her life, Perdita eyed me fearfully from under Anita's chair. She prattled on and on about how she and Roger had met in the park, a story I already knew, but I sat there suffering as she gushed, filling in the details. "Cruella, you will simply love Roger. He's such a talented composer," she said, smiling at me. "I have to tell you how we met. If you can believe it, I hated him at first. His dog, Pongo, was acting up at the park, trying to get Perdita's attention, and there was Roger chasing after him like some kind of fool, getting Pongo's leash tangled in with Perdita's, making us both fall into the water. It was hilarious."

"That sounds very romantic," I said, not meaning a word of it.

"It was. It was like out of one of our stories, Cruella. Remember how Princess Tulip was annoyed by Prince, oh, what was his name again?"

"Prince Popinjay," I said. "I think that was his name."

"Yes! Remember how Tulip didn't like him at first, but after a while they fell in love? Well, it was like that. For both me and Perdita." All of this was sickening to me. As I was sitting there listening to her story, I found myself more and more distracted by that feeling that was washing over me. "But of course, I am being insensitive. I heard about your Jack. I am so sorry, Cruella," she said. Instead of warmth and comfort, I just felt cold. Empty.

Somehow, reconnecting with Anita was no longer important. I didn't understand it at first, how something so important to me could suddenly evaporate. Before I got ready to leave Hell Hall I had been so full of hope for a fresh start with Anita. I had tricked myself into thinking we would easily fall back into friendship again, even sisterhood. I don't know what possessed me. It was as if I was under the same spell that had overtaken me at Christmastime so many years before, when Anita had bewitched me into thinking my mama was a scheming, evil person. When she convinced me that my servants loved me more than my own dear mama. As I sat there listening to how wonderful Anita's life was, I became sure I must have temporarily lost my senses when I'd decided to call her. My distaste for her intensified as I sat there listening to her prattle on and on about Roger and Pongo, hardly even acknowledging my loss or even aware that hearing her talk about that fool Roger would make me miss my Jack. And the more she talked, the more I despised her, *and* her stupid dog. Neither of them loved me anymore. Perdita didn't even know me. Mama had been right about her. She was simple, common, and unworthy of my friendship.

I wanted to hurt her, like she'd hurt me. I wanted to do something to show I wasn't someone to be pitied. I wanted to make something of my life, something spectacular, and make my mother proud of me again. It was all I could think about. I was obsessed.

Sitting there with Anita and Perdita was just wasting time. I had to come up with a plan. Some way to distinguish myself the way my mother had always wanted me to. But how? How would I do that?

"Cruella, are you okay? You seem to be lost in thought," said Anita.

"I'm sorry, Anita, I suppose I'm just a little sad Perdita doesn't remember me," I said, grasping at something that sounded believable.

And then the beast growled at me.

"I'm sorry, Cruella. She's usually very sweet. I don't know why she's being this way. Perhaps she's just feeling particularly vulnerable around strangers because of her condition."

"What?" I said. "Her condition?"

"The puppies, Cruella. She's due quite soon, I'm afraid."

"Perdita is having puppies?" I blinked. And then it came to me. A way to get my revenge. A way to hurt Anita *and* her stupid dog, Perdita. A way to distinguish myself.

I finally had a way to make my mother proud.

Nothing else mattered now.

## CHAPTER XIX

# ᛏ BLAME THE
# HENCHMEN

ᛏ blame Horace and Jasper. My plan would have worked if it weren't for them. Honestly, I suppose it's my fault for hiring such simpleminded fools. Next time I'll know better than to hire shifty-looking men from a back alley. What did I expect? It's not like you can check references when hiring henchmen, now can you? It's not as if you can call their previous employer and ask if they did their misdeeds well. But they really did make a cock-up of everything. Well, my adoring fans know the truth. Even if the newspapers tell another story. Even if they paint me as a maniac in all the rags.

Yes, there was a car crash.

## I Blame the Henchmen

Yes, the puppies got away.

But I have another plan. A *better* plan. A plan that will work this time. And I will do it without those fool henchmen. I will succeed! It's an utterly brilliant idea, and the Radcliffes, well, they're playing right into my hands, aren't they? Gathering those dogs together all in one place.

But we're jumping ahead. I know what you want to hear about. Well, let me tell you my version of the story.

✤ ✤ ✤ ✤

As I drove home after having coffee with Anita I became more livid. And as that anger grew I saw everything more clearly. I won't lament over my muddled thinking before. I won't question why. None of that matters. My only regret was doubting my mama. She was the most magnificent woman I have ever known. Self-possessed, beautiful, rich, and always dripping in furs. She showed me how much she loved me by giving me furs for as long as I could remember. And always with the same message. *Distinguish yourself.* Well, I decided I would, and I would redeem myself in her eyes—for the times I drifted away from her and doubted her. I would finally be able to show her my love the way she had shown me hers. And I would show her I was a strong, capable woman, just like her, able to survive even the greatest of heartbreak and misfortune. And if I happened to take down my enemies in the process, well, simply splendid.

And I still will! Just because those dolts ruined everything the first time around doesn't mean a thing! I never should have trusted them with the job in the first place. I can't believe I gave those idiots the rest of my money to buy every Dalmatian puppy in every shop, only for them to lose them along with Perdita, Pongo, and their puppies! Perdita was rightfully mine, and so were her spotted little beasts!

Never mind. I will wait. I will wait until the time is right. I was in too much of a hurry. I see that now. And I should have kept a closer eye on those fools. I should never have left them and those puppies alone in Hell Hall. But I couldn't wait. I had to tell Mama what I had in mind. I had to tell her I would finally make her grandest wish come true. I made mistakes. I should never have left those fools alone in Hell Hall and I should never have gone to my mother empty-handed. I shouldn't have told her my plan before it was complete. I see that now. I've learned my lesson.

I mean, darlings, you've already read about it in all the papers, haven't you? It would be boring for me to tell you about it. But let's say you don't read the trash rags, or have somehow never picked up a newspaper in your life or seen my face splashed all over the news. Let's say you haven't seen those tearful interviews with Anita and her fool Roger recounting how I came swooping into their lives and stole their puppies. I know you have, but for argument's sake, I'll tell you anyway.

I called Anita shortly after our coffee date and I told her everything I had originally planned to tell her that day. How she was right. How I detested my mama. How she'd taken everything from me. Not that I meant a word of it, mind you. But I had to make her believe. I told her to make her sweet, simple soul sorry for me. I wanted those puppies. And who better to give them to than a brokenhearted, abandoned widow? As I predicted, Anita agreed that I could have them. She always was a simple fool.

But I made a tragic mistake.

I went by the house to say hello and check on Perdita's progress. I should *never* have tried to pretend Anita and I were still friends. What I could hide easily on the phone was impossible to conceal in person. My contempt for her, Roger, and their stupid dogs was written on my face from the minute I first looked at their dull faces. I couldn't stand to be in their hovel of a house—and Roger knew it.

At the time I thought I'd played my role remarkably well. I was the sad, lonely wretch I needed to be so she would feel sorry for me and give me those puppies. I played the roll magnificently. I stood on the doorstep, ready to make my grand entrance, when I heard voices from inside.

That fool Roger was singing! Oh, it was too

much, *too much* I tell you. Then I heard the words to the song. He was singing about me!

*Evil Thing? Evil Thing*, can you believe it?

Rage seethed through me. Well, I would show them. I would give the grandest performance of my life!

And then it happened. I rang the bell, and who opened the door but Mrs. Baddeley! I was only momentarily thrown off by seeing the dumpy woman standing in Anita's doorway. Was this the servant she had told me about in her letters? The one they called Nanny? They didn't have children! Anita must still look to her as some sort of mother figure. Oh, who knows. Who cares? Not me. I pretended not to recognize the fool, pushing her aside and focusing my gaze on Anita. It was the best, most spectacular entrance I had ever made.

I swooped right into Anita and Roger's. I walked into that house and I was ravishing. Black dress, jade jewelry, my white fur coat lined in red, and red shoes!

"Anita, darling!" I said, my arms outstretched.

I really was too much. Too much fabulousness for that little hovel.

"How are you?" asked the little woman in her little house, her voice as soft and timid as a mouse. Ha! I rhymed! And better than that Roger does in his silly jingles. Of course I'd heard Roger's insipid song about me while I was standing on their doorstep, and I'd heard their conversation. So Anita told Roger how I'd watched after her in school. How I'd defended her. He called me her *dearly devoted schoolmate*, and so I was. Now I was going to call in on that friendship. It was time she repaid me for all the trouble I'd gotten into standing up for her. Time I was repaid for all those nights she lived at my house, ate my food, and grew close to my servants. Time I was repaid for them loving her more than they loved me.

And then I remembered. I was supposed to be striking a tragic figure, not an impossibly magnificent one. I thought I'd better tone it down. I had to remember I was the grieving, abandoned widow, after all. I was lonely and sad and needed puppies to bring cheer to my dreary, empty life.

"Miserable, darling, as usual. Perfectly wretched," I said. I had to keep up appearances, didn't I? Perdita was nowhere to be seen, and that goofy-faced Pongo was under my feet as I searched their little flat, trying to find the wretched beast.

"Where are they? Where are they? For heavens' sakes, where are they?" Where was Perdita? I couldn't find her, and I didn't see a solitary puppy anywhere. I was promised puppies! How was I going to distinguish myself without those damn puppies? Oh this was a mess.

"Who, Cruella? I don't—" Anita began.

*Who? Who? Who in hell do you think I mean?* I thought. My goodness, what an idiot Anita had turned into. And it was no wonder with all the racket coming down from the attic. That damnable horn-blowing fool was up there making a menace of himself. I have no idea how Anita lived with such a horrible man!

"The puppies, the puppies!" I said. "No time for games. Where are the little brutes?" I almost let the puppy out of the bag with that one. *Cruella, watch yourself. Anita needs to think you want to love and protect the beasts.*

"Oh! It'll be at least three weeks. No rushing these things, you know," she said, not even blinking an eye. Maybe she hadn't heard me call them brutes. Roger was playing his music so loudly I could barely hear myself think.

"Anita, you're such a wit," I said, deciding I needed to butter her and that wretched Pongo up. "Here, dog, here. Here, dog." But the beast only growled at me.

"Cruella, isn't that a new fur coat?" asked Anita. I guess it was new to her. It was the coat Mama had gotten me for my twenty-fifth birthday. But I wasn't going to tell her that. As far as Anita knew I now hated my mama.

"My only true love, darling. I live for furs. I *worship* furs. After all, is there a woman in all this wretched world who doesn't?" And it was true. My plan was coming together even more as I heard my own words. There wasn't a woman alive who didn't love furs, and my mother was clearly no exception.

She loved them even more than I did. *Good grief,* I thought. *Does that horrible man have to play his horn so loudly?* It really was getting on my nerves.

"Oh, I'd like a nice fur, but there are so many other things—" Anita started to say, but I cut her off.

"Sweet, simple Anita. I know, I know! This horrid little house is your dream castle," I said. "And poor Roger is your bold and fearless Sir Galahad!" I said, laughing.

"Oh, Cruella," Anita said quietly. I knew that tone. It was the one she used when I had gone too far. She used it all throughout our childhood, the condescending little twit. But I had forgotten myself. *Don't be a fool, Cruella. Don't mess this up. Pick another topic. Say something sweet.*

"And then of course you have your little spotted friends," I said, transfixed by a photo of Pongo and Perdita. "Oh yes. Yes, I must say, such perfectly beautiful coats." I had to get out of there before Anita realized what I was up to. It was clear Pongo didn't trust me, and I have to admit, I found it difficult playing my role. It was like the day when I had yelled at Jackson and my mama, after Jack died. I'd seen myself acting out, saying things I hadn't intended, but I couldn't help myself. The same thing was happening with Anita. I'd have it in my head to say something sweet to her, say something kind about that fool Roger, but when I opened my mouth only the truth came out. I had no idea what was happening to me. It was maddening.

"Won't you have some tea, Cruella?" Anita asked. But I had to go. If I stayed one more moment she was going to catch on.

"No, I've got to run, darling. Now let me know when the puppies arrive. You will, won't you, dear?"

"Yes, Cruella," Anita said, like the good girl she was. She never could say no to me.

"Now, don't forget it's a promise," I said, and I left as quickly as I could. "See you in three weeks. Cheerio. Cheerio, darling!"

The plan started out well enough, wouldn't you say? Even with my little blunders I had that stupid Anita eating out of the palm of my hand. I'd seen where she lived. It was worse than I had imagined. There was no way she could afford two dogs and their puppies, and she would never go back on a promise. She wasn't the sort. Besides, Perdita was mine. The least she could do was give me her puppies. Everything was going exactly as I had planned.

## Chapter XX

# A Wild and
# Stormy Night

Anita called me at Hell Hall early one evening about three weeks later to let me know the puppies were arriving. She seemed like she regretted saying I could have them. Like she was trying to figure out how to wriggle her way out of her promise. Well, I wasn't going to let her. I drove over there straightaway. Even if I couldn't have the puppies that evening, and I had to wait until they were old enough to leave their mother, I still wanted to see them. They were mine! Mine, I say.

Mrs. Baddeley let me into the house and showed me to the living room before she ran off to the kitchen to rejoin Roger and Anita. I do believe she was afraid to be alone in the room with me! I paced in the living room, waiting for my puppies to be born while everyone else fretted and cooed over Perdita and Pongo. And then I heard the news. I heard Mrs. Baddeley's bellowing from the living room. "The puppies! The puppies are here!" she yelled. And then came Roger's voice.

"How many?"

*Eight?* Did I hear her say there were eight puppies? My goodness. What I could do with eight puppies. It was going even better than I planned. *Eight puppies.* And then the woman bellowed again.

"Ten!" *Ten puppies.* I couldn't believe it. I continued to pace in the living room, but I could hear everything going on in the kitchen.

"Eleven!" yelled Mrs. Baddeley, and the number of puppies kept rising. Now this was even better than I'd hoped for. It was a miracle! I waited for what felt like an eternity for everyone to come out of the kitchen. They were whispering in there about something. They were talking in hushed tones; I could hardly hear them. And then I heard it. *Fifteen puppies*. I couldn't wait any longer. I had to see them.

"Fifteen puppies! Fifteen puppies! How marvelous, how marvelous, how perfectly . . . Ugh." Wait. Something wasn't right. They didn't have their spots! Anyone could make a white fur coat. Even *I* had one of those, for heaven's sake. I wanted spotted fur! It had to be spotted; it had to be special! I was robbed! I was lied to! What had that Perdita been up to? White puppies, indeed. "Oh, the devil take it, they're mongrels, no spots! No spots at all. What a horrid little white rat!" I said, looking at the ugly creature in Mrs. Baddeley's arms.

"They're not mongrels!" yelled Mrs. Baddeley. "They'll get their spots. Just you wait and see!"

"That's right, Cruella. They'll have their spots in a few weeks," said Anita, coming out of the washroom.

"Oh, well in that case, I'll take them all. The whole litter. Just name your price, dear," I said. I knew she was only expecting me to want a few of them. She had promised me the litter before she knew how many puppies Perdita was carrying. Well, I intended to take them all.

Anita looked pained. "I'm afraid we can't give them up. Poor Perdita, she'd be heartbroken."

She'd changed her mind. She went back on her promise! I was livid, but I tried to play it cool.

"Anita, don't be ridiculous. You can't possibly afford to keep them. You can scarcely afford to feed yourselves," I said. But Anita wasn't budging.

"I'm sure we'll get along," she said, her mind made up.

"Yes, I know. I know. Roger's . . . Roger's *songs*!" I couldn't stop laughing. "Oh, now really, enough of this nonsense. I'll pay you twice what they're worth. Come now, I'm being more than generous." I took out my checkbook, even though I barely had two quid to rub together. "Blast this pen! Blast this wretched, wretched pen, ah!" It was really quite funny, when I think of it now. The ink sprayed all over Roger. "When can the puppies leave their mother? Two weeks? Three weeks?" I asked. I could hardly wait.

"Never." It was Roger. He'd found his voice. That stammering fool said he wasn't going to give me a single puppy! I had to ask Anita if he was serious. I mean, really, how can you take such a man seriously? He was a joke. A laughingstock. Imagine, a man like him trying to stand up to *me*. And Anita? Well, if she wanted to be a fool's dishrag then that was her misfortune. I was through with her. Through with *all of them*.

"I'll get even. Just wait. You'll be sorry, you fools! You *idiots*!"

## CHAPTER XXI

# ONE HUNDRED AND ONE DALMATIANS

My henchmen, Horace and Jasper, told me all about it. How they locked that idiot Mrs. Baddeley up in the attic and took the puppies. She always was an old fool, and now she was an even older fool than before. They tricked the old woman, not that it took much trickery on their part. They waited until Anita and Roger took Perdita and Pongo for a walk, then simply rang the doorbell and made up a lie, pretending they were there to fix the electric or gas or something. Simple. And oh, what a stir it made. You'd think someone had kidnapped the Queen the way everyone was acting. It was in all the papers! And it really was very amusing, seeing Anita and

Roger's photos. Reading that frumpy old woman's account of the story. I laughed when I read all the headlines. I couldn't help myself. I mean really. Such a fuss over a bunch of puppies. I was staying in a hotel in London, Mama's treat. She was in town staying at the same hotel, and we were meeting for dinner. I just had to tell her about my plans. I couldn't wait to see the look on her face when I told her what I was up to. What I had in mind. My master plan. Oh, it was too divine. She would be so proud of me.

I had it all planned out. I had those fool henchmen staying in Hell Hall with the puppies while I was tucked safely away in my hotel room. There was no way I was going to be connected to those puppies or those idiots Horace and Jasper if Scotland Yard came poking around. Thank goodness Mama was in town.

But the papers. Oh, the papers. They were a gas! I read them in bed, taking delight in everyone's misery while I was waiting for my hair to set. I had a marvelous evening planned with my mama and I wanted to look my best.

"Dognapping! Tsk, tsk. Can you imagine such a thing? Fifteen puppies stolen. But they are darling little things." I was suffering from fits of laughter. "Anita and her bashful Beethoven. Pipe and all! Oh, Roger, you are a fool!" I honestly couldn't remember when I'd felt better. It was all too delicious. It was the most delightful evening I'd had in ages, since Jack was alive. It was all too wonderful. I had the puppies hidden away at Hell Hall, and I thought I had gotten away with it! My revenge on Anita and her fool of a husband. Saying no to me! Making up wretched songs about me. Me! Cruella De Vil! I'd taught them a lesson they would never forget. Maybe I would send Anita a little coat, as a thank-you gift. She'd said she would like one, after all. But of course that jumped-up musician of hers couldn't afford to buy her one. Why not send her a little gift? Oh, she'd lost her chance at a wonderful life, traveling the world with me!

But I mustn't dwell in the past. I thought everything was going brilliantly, and I couldn't wait to tell Mama what I was up to. She would be so proud of me! Her daughter, the first ever to make fur coats out of spotted puppies. And she would adore it! She'd wanted a muffler all those years ago, and this would be so much more magnificent. Everything was going brilliantly.

Of course I didn't much care for having Scotland Yard investigate me, calling me in for questioning. Me! I know it was Roger who sent them sniffing around me. They had posters plastered all over the city, and the newspapers were splashed with those puppies and those fools' faces. Between that and Scotland Yard taking an interest in the case, those imbeciles Jasper and Horace were nervous.

They called me at the hotel even though I had forbade them. I thought it was Mama calling me to confirm our dinner later, but it was Jasper.

"Hello? Jasper, Jasper you idiot! How dare you call here?" I couldn't believe he was calling me at the hotel. Simpleminded ghoul that he was, he couldn't follow even the simplest of instructions.

"But we don't want no more of this, we want our boodle!" This was too much. Just too much. Did I really have to hold their hands while I was trying to get ready for an evening out with my mama? Why on earth was I paying these idiots from what little I had left?

"Not one shilling until the job's done. Do you understand?" I said. There was no way I was going to pay them for a job half done! But they wouldn't relent.

"It's here in the blinking papers, pictures and all!"

"Hang the papers! It'll be forgotten tomorrow," I said. And it was true. Who cared about a bunch of puppies anyway? Tomorrow the world would find something else to get upset over.

"Ah, shut up, you idiot!" he said. I couldn't believe it!

"What?"

"Oh no! Not you, miss. I mean Horace here."

"Why, you imbecile!" And I hung up the phone. This was all too much. Too much. I decided I'd better call Anita and see if there was anything to Jasper's anxiety.

These idiotic henchmen were playing havoc with my nerves. This was the last thing I needed before I met Mama. The last thing. Someone finally answered the phone. It was that ridiculous stammering Roger.

"Hello, hello, Inspector?" he stammered. Ah, so they had been speaking to the inspector!

"Is Anita there?" I asked.

"Who?" he asked. My stars, what a fool!

"Anita!"

"Oh, it's for you," he said coldly, passing the phone to Anita. Her sweet voice was a nice change from Roger's accusatory tone.

"Hello?"

"Anita, darling!"

"Oh, Cruella." She did not sound happy to hear from me.

"Oh, Anita, what a dreadful thing. I just saw the papers. I couldn't believe it."

"Yes, Cruella, it was quite a shock. Roger, please!" That fool must have been chattering in her ear during our entire conversation. I didn't hear what he was saying, but I'm guessing it wasn't anything nice. "Yes, yes, we're doing everything possible," she said.

"Have you called the police?"

"Yes, we called Scotland Yard. But I'm afraid . . ."

And then that horrid man took the phone from Anita. *"Where are they?"* he demanded. And then it was Anita again.

"You idiot!" she exclaimed.

"Anita!"

"Sorry, Cruella." Oh, she had been talking to Roger. That made me smile. I asked if they would keep me informed about their little drama. "Yes, if there is any news we'll let you know. Thank you, Cruella."

Ha! Clearly she thought Roger was an idiot as well. I was happy to see she was on my side.

We were fine. They had no leads. Scotland Yard wouldn't be bothering me again. Horace and Jasper had nothing to worry about. *I* had nothing to worry about. Except for one thing: what was I going to do with just fifteen puppies? That wouldn't even make the muffler Mama was so keen on. I needed more. *Many* more. And the last thing I needed was to be seen buying up every last puppy in London.

No, I needed those wretched men just a little longer. And I needed more puppies.

❖ ❖ ❖ ❖

Fools that they were, Jasper and Horace managed to buy every Dalmatian puppy they could get their hands on. It took all the money I had. There wasn't a single puppy left, not in all of London. They were all mine! They called the hotel from the pay phone in the village again as I was heading down to meet my mama in the hotel restaurant. I was ecstatic. One hundred and one Dalmatians! I would be able to make Mama the most marvelous coat imaginable. It would be like the day I gave her Papa's money. I imagined her smile when she saw it. I imagined her telling me she loved me again. Come to think of it, with so many puppies I'd be able to make one for myself as well. Maybe even one day I could be a fur mogul. I would rule the fashion world! Mama loves fashion. She adores it more than anything. She would be so proud of me. I was proud of myself, too. What started out as a desire to make my mama something she would love turned into something bigger. Much bigger. Something magnificent. I couldn't wait to share my news with my mama.

She would be so proud that I had finally found a way to distinguish myself.

✤ ✤ ✤ ✤

My dinner with Mama was a disaster. Everything went terribly wrong. It was my fault, really. I should have waited until I had the coat made for her. Perhaps then she would have understood. But as it was, it all went terribly, terribly wrong.

We met at the Criterion, her favorite restaurant, for dinner. It was a place out of antiquity: lavish, beautiful, and everything my mother represented to me, with its gilded rooms and splendid chandeliers. It was so heavenly to be going to such a place again. To be surrounded by beauty and opulence, and not the squalor and decay of Hell Hall. My mother looked beautiful in her lovely gold-beaded dress, and she was covered in diamonds, around her neck, on her wrists, and on many of her fingers. She even had diamond hairpins arranged in her elaborate updo. She was sparkling. I was wearing my signature outfit: my slinky black dress, my jade jewelry, and of course my fur coat. She was already seated when I arrived. All eyes turned to me as I was escorted by the maître d' to Mama's table. She looked quite shocked at the sight of me, as did most everyone else in the room. I know I looked stunning that evening, but can't a woman meet her mother for dinner without people ogling her? I mean, really! I know I was something of an it girl during my days with Jack, but this was really too much.

Finally, I sat down with Mama.

"Cruella! Are you quite well?" she asked.

"Yes, Mama, I am. You look lovely this evening."

"Thank you, my dear. You look, well . . . *interesting*, to say the least."

"I do hope you think so! I have such wonderful news to share with you. But let's order before I share my news," I said.

"Cruella, my dear, I'm not convinced you should

be out," she said, glancing around as the other guests stared and whispered.

"Oh, I'm used to people looking at me, Mama. Everywhere I go people are staring. Jack and I made quite the splash in the papers in our day."

"Cruella, you are so thin and pale, my darling. You look like you haven't slept in weeks. And your hair, it's so . . . *wild*. You don't look at all well. I think we'd better go."

"No, Mama! I have to share my news with you," I said. "We can't go, not yet."

"What's your news then, darling?" she asked, her eyes shifting from me to the other diners still gawking at us. Well, I had had it. I wasn't going to let those star chasers ruin my evening. They were making my mama uncomfortable. And I wasn't going to stand for it any longer. I stood up, raising my hands and voice so everyone would pay attention. "Will you please divert your attention from me and focus on your own meals and conversations?" I said, while Mama protested.

"Cruella, do sit down! You're making a scene."

"No, Mama, *they're* making a scene!" I said. "They're all ruining our special evening! This is London for goodness' sake! It's not as if they've not seen a socialite before! They should behave themselves and try using just a modicum of decorum." My mama was mortified.

"Cruella, stop this at once," she said, raising her voice and gripping my arm tightly, forcing me to sit down. "Cruella, stop this! What did you expect, coming out looking the way you do? You look ghastly. I mean, really, Cruella. You're still wearing that dress! It's morbid! And look, it's hanging off of you. You look a fright, like a skeleton in rags. *That* is why everyone is looking at you. Now, please, let's leave."

"But Mama, I want to share my plan. You're going to be so proud of me. I have the most *splendid* plan. You remember Perdita, that horrible dog Papa gave me? Well, Mama, she has had puppies! Puppies! Isn't it a scream? And I remembered your suggestion about using her fur for a muffler, so . . . well, Mama, I'm going to do just that! I am going to have the most splendid fur coat made for you! Oh, you will love it, Mama! I know you will! And you will be so proud!"

My mother's voice grew quiet. "Cruella, my dear. Stop this at once. I won't hear another word."

"But Mama!" I said, standing up. "I know, I know! I ruined the surprise! I should have waited until the coat was finished. But I swear you will love it. I know you will be so proud of me!" I must have raised my voice more than I realized, because everyone in the room looked mesmerized by me. Even the staff were rushing over to listen to my declaration. Then something shifted in my mama. She seemed to realize how wonderful my idea really was. She spoke to me in the calmest and sweetest voice.

"Yes, Cruella, dear. That is a dazzling idea. I am very proud of you, but we must leave. You're far too famous to be out in public. We're causing something of a stir, and I don't want the local rags to get their hands on your idea before you're able to execute it." She looked around the room nervously. Just then a tall man came up with our coats, and he ushered us out of the restaurant and onto the street.

"Your car will be here shortly, Lady De Vil," he said.

"Please arrange a cab for my daughter," she said.

"But Mama, I thought I would go back with you to the hotel. Besides, I have my car, I can follow you there."

"No, my dear. I don't think you should be driving. Please, let me get you into a cab, and I will arrange to have someone bring your car around to Hell Hall, I mean, De Vil Hall in the morning."

"What was that, Mama?"

"Nothing, dear," she said. But I knew she must have heard the rumors about my estate, what they were calling it. "Do as Mama says, and get yourself straight home and into bed. I will pay for the cab. And Cruella, stay at home and rest, won't you, dear? Don't go out. Stay put. I will send someone around in a day or two to check on you."

"Mama, I am fine. Please don't worry."

"Cruella, do as I say! Now, I have to go. Don't

disobey me," she said, blowing me a kiss and getting into her car.

✦ ✦ ✦ ✦

I think she misread my excitement for something else. Something else entirely. And I wasn't sure she understood my plans. She was so worried about me getting swarmed by fans, I'm not sure she was listening properly. Well, I would make it up to her. I would have her coat made before she left London. Then she would see. But I was running out of time.

She would only be in London for so long, so I had to do it right then. After she left, I insisted they give me my car, and I drove all the way back to Hell Hall and told Horace and Jasper the police were onto us. It was all lies, of course. I told them the police were everywhere and we had to kill the puppies right away. It was the only way I could get them to do the deed quickly. Simple men that they were, they had no idea how to go about slaughtering a bunch of puppies. I didn't care how they did it. I just wanted it done. I needed those puppies. I still do.

"Poison them, drown them, bash them in the head! I don't care how you kill the little beasts. I just want it done. The police are everywhere," I added for a bit of drama. I needed to get those fools off their bottoms.

They were glued to the television. Transfixed by a show called *What's My Crime?* A TV show! *A TV show!* Bloody fools. I had to slap some sense into them. I needed those puppies murdered. I needed them skinned. I needed to have my mama's coat made. Oh yes. She would love me again. She would. I was sure of it. "Listen, you idiots. I'll be back first thing in the morning. The job better be done or I'll call the police! Do you understand?" I needed to rattle their cages. Of course I wouldn't call the police. Why would I? But those two were not the brightest. Thank goodness they believed me.

Of course, the job never did get done. It just goes to show you that if you want something done right, you have to do it yourself.

It all went terribly wrong from there, didn't it? You know the story. You saw my photo in the paper. And I'm sure you saw Horace and Jasper blab about the entire debacle when they made their appearance on their favorite show, *What's My Crime?* Those stupid morons prattled on and on, describing the events in lurid detail. How we chased those puppies on that treacherously winding road; how I gripped the wheel, my eyes blazing with madness as they ran me off the road; and finally, how I crashed my car, letting those wretched dogs escape! The reenactment of me on that damnable TV show in my wrecked car was laughable. It made me out to be some sort of madwoman with wild, swirling eyes. A deranged, screaming lunatic. Well, that's not the real story, duckies.

That show and those fools made a mockery of me. It might have made for good television, but it didn't show how I was *really* feeling. It wasn't madness that overcame me. It wasn't even anger. It was heartbreak, disappointment, and loss. It was heartache. As my car careened over that cliff I felt my life crashing down around me. Everything was in ruins. And I was in despair. I thought I had lost my final chance to make my mama love me again. To make her proud of me.

But fear not, adoring readers. As I sit here in Hell Hall, my plan for revenge shines like a star in the darkness. It has become my only solace. My greatest source of hope for happiness, and for reconciliation with Mama.

The Radcliffes haven't beaten me. No. I have a new plan. A better plan, and it involves all those dogs Anita and Roger are hoarding on that estate they bought with all the money they made on that horrible song about me. Oh, I know you've heard it. "Vampire bat" indeed! They think they can make a fool of me? Well, I will show them an "inhuman beast"! And they will see what an "evil thing" I can be! I will have my revenge. Mark my words, darlings. I am Cruella De Vil!

But this time . . . this time it will be different. I will have to be patient. I will have to wait. No, I can't rush things. I have to take my time. Anita and Roger have ninety-nine puppies living on their stupid little farm, and of course there are Perdita and Pongo. And *I will* have those dogs! Just imagine how much more fur I will have after waiting for those puppies to become fully grown. Imagine all the coats I will make, and how happy Mama will be when I give them *all to her*. Then she will love me again. I am sure of it.

# AFTERWORD

$\mathcal{D}$ear readers,

I thought it would comfort you to know that Anita and Roger, along with Mrs. Baddeley, Perdita, Pongo, and their brood of ninety-nine Dalmatian puppies, are all quite safe. And you can take even further comfort in knowing they are all living happily on the royalties from Roger's hit song, "Cruella De Vil." If that isn't irony, then I don't know what is.

It has been a most unsettling experience writing Cruella's memoir. I spent months locked up with her in Hell Hall, taking down her story. I have changed nothing. Everything you read here is what she told me, word for word, night after night. I listened to rants and ravings and suffering through her fits of endless, terrifying laughter.

Hell Hall is a cold, eerie place that lives up to its name. That is where Cruella De Vil now lives, locked away by her mother, who scarcely visits. Lady De Vil's old head housekeeper, Mrs. Web, watches over her. Cruella's mother was horrified that fateful night at dinner, when Cruella shared her plans to make a coat out of Dalmatian puppies. But even more terrifying to her mother was the scandal Cruella caused. You might recall that photo in the papers of Cruella with bloodshot eyes full of hate and fury. Her mother felt she brought shame on her family, not to mention her social standing. So her mother had her locked away, with the Spider.

I have often wondered if Cruella really hated Mrs. Web from the moment she met her, like she claims. Somehow I doubt it. Don't mistake me, Mrs. Web is a cold woman. Cruella's descriptions of her are not exaggerated. For the record, the woman reminds me, too, of a sinister spider. But I can't help wondering if Cruella's current circumstances haven't clouded her memory of the woman. Still, even the most austere of women eventually reach their breaking point. To quiet her ranting, Mrs. Web felt it would help if Cruella had the opportunity to tell her side of the story. Mrs. Web had read the previous books in my Villains series, and thought I would be the right person to transcribe Cruella's tale. And so I came to Hell Hall.

It is not my place to tell you what to think of Cruella De Vil and the events that led her to be locked up in Hell Hall. But I can tell you this: I listened to her story. And I felt sorry for her. And for a moment, just a moment, mind you, I finally came to understand why she wanted to kill those puppies. And why she still wants to, to this this day. I've spent sleepless nights wondering how things could have gone differently for Cruella. I wonder what would have happened if Cruella's father hadn't died, if her mother had never left her. I wonder what would have happened if Anita had agreed to travel the world with her. And I wonder if it would have made a difference if Sir Huntley had managed to talk her into keeping her money. Would she still be locked up today? Would she be plotting the murder of one hundred and one Dalmatians?

And then I wonder if those earrings really *are* cursed. Perhaps they changed her every time she put them on. Perhaps they didn't. We will never know. But what I do know is that she won't take them off. She wears them still, every day, along with that slinky black dress and the jade ring given to her by her beloved Crackerjack.

Whatever caused Cruella's descent into darkness and delirium, I couldn't stand the idea of her being locked away in Hell Hall with her most hated childhood servant. Of course I realize the beastly woman can never be released. But does Cruella really deserve to live the rest of her days locked away without a single person who loves or cares for her? Isn't that how she became the woman she is?

Maybe you won't agree with me; maybe you won't think she deserves just a little bit of happiness, but I called Miss Pricket, her old governess. I told her about Cruella's circumstances, and she graciously agreed to come help care for Cruella. She arrived on my last day in Hell Hall, and she looked exactly as Cruella had described, just a little older. I could tell Miss Pricket still loved her even after everything Cruella had put her through. I could tell she still saw Cruella as a sad lonely little girl, and there is a part of me that does as well.

In the end, everything isn't always as black-and-white as the markings on a Dalmatian puppy. Even for an evil thing like Cruella De Vil.

Sincerely,

*Serena Valentino*

Serena Valentino